"I'm here for ou~~r a~~ppointment," Caitlin said brightly.

"I don't think so," Devon answered.

Caitlin blinked at the terse statement, but decided to ignore it. She focused again on the man beside the door. "I'm an image consultant. I explained that to your secretary on the phone."

If anything, he looked more skeptical. "So you go door-to-door, selling makeup?"

Caitlin bristled. She didn't know what kind of game Devon Walsh was playing, or why he was pretending to be ignorant of their appointment, but she knew one thing. The guy needed a personality makeover more than a haircut.

"No. Our meeting was to discuss the essay Jennifer wrote for the contest."

The girl peeking out from behind Devon's legs let out a tiny gasp, but her father didn't seem to notice.

The wariness in Devon's eyes turned to confusion. "Contest?"

"The makeover contest for *Twin City Trends* magazine."

"Let me get this straight. Are you telling me that Jenny entered a makeover contest?"

"No—"

"Well, that's a relief."

"She entered you."

KATHRYN SPRINGER

is a lifelong Wisconsin resident. Growing up in a "newspaper" family, she spent long hours as a child plunking out stories on her mother's typewriter and hasn't stopped writing since! She loves to write inspirational romance because it allows her to combine her faith in God with her love of a happy ending.

Family Treasures
Kathryn Springer

Steeple
Hill®

Published by Steeple Hill Books™

STEEPLE HILL BOOKS

Steeple
Hill®

ISBN-13: 978-0-373-87505-4
ISBN-10:   0-373-87505-3

FAMILY TREASURES

By wisdom a house is built, and through understanding it is established; through knowledge its rooms are filled with rare and beautiful treasures.

—*Proverbs* 24:3–4

To Mom…who faithfully (and patiently) tweaks my manuscripts, finds lost words and always knows when to use "affect" instead of "effect" (someday I'll get it right!). You go above and beyond the call of duty, and your encouragement and enthusiasm keep me pressing on.

Chapter One

Another Monday.

And if the early morning traffic jam and the ten voice-mail messages waiting for her attention weren't *enough* proof it was Monday, Caitlin McBride knew she could add the three grueling hours she'd just spent shopping with the daughter of one of her clients. What should have been a fairly easy search for the perfect "little black dress" had quickly turned into a battle of wills when the teenager revealed that she *did* like the color black—but only as the background for hundreds of tiny skulls.

Caitlin had won in the end—she always did—but at the moment she needed to rebound with a cup of strong coffee and the piece of dark chocolate tucked away in her desk drawer.

She didn't break stride as she swept past her assistant's desk. "Sabrina, I have an appointment with Dawn Gallagher at Twin City Trends this afternoon. Don't forget to leave the entries for the makeover contest on my desk before you take your lunch break."

"Um, Ms. McBride?"

Judging from the undercurrent of misery in Sabrina Buckley's voice, the chocolate was going to have to wait.

Caitlin paused and pivoted slowly on one stiletto heel. "Yes?"

"I'm, ah, having a little…trouble with the elimination round."

Caitlin sighed. Why leadership seminars continued to claim that "delegating responsibility" was a positive thing, she didn't know.

"What kind of trouble?"

"Well, you told me to divide the entries into two piles." Sabrina gestured to the overflowing bins on her desk. "One for women who already look like models and just want to be featured in a magazine. And one for average, everyday-looking women who could potentially bring new clients to IMAGEine after their makeover."

"That's right. Two piles." The toe of Caitlin's shoe tapped against the plush carpeting. "So what seems to be the problem?"

"This one." Sabrina held out a photograph. "It doesn't exactly fall into either…category."

"Of course it does," Caitlin said firmly, retracing her steps back to the reception desk. "Let me see…."

That.

The sentence ended in something that sounded suspiciously like a gurgle.

"It's a…man."

Her assistant grinned. "It certainly is."

Caitlin ignored the sudden, irreverent sparkle in Sabrina's eyes as she studied the photo and made a swift assessment of the subject's rugged masculine features. Fathomless dark eyes. Arrogant jaw. A shaggy mane of hair the color of espresso.

Perfect cheekbones…

"*He* sent in an essay?"

"Not exactly him. No." Sabrina squirmed briefly in her chair.

Caitlin exhaled and counted to five. Out loud. And then she tried again. "But he entered the contest?"

"Not exactly him. No."

"Sabrina—" Caitlin's eyes narrowed.

"I'll show you." Sabrina's hand disappeared into the pile of papers and she unearthed an entry form, waving it in front of Caitlin like a white flag. "You have to read this. Then it will make sense." The young woman nibbled on the tip of her ragged fingernail. "Maybe."

"Fine." Caitlin felt a tension headache sink its hooks into the base of her neck as she plucked the paperwork and the photo out of Sabrina's hands. "Let me know when my next appointment arrives."

"Yes, Ms. McBride."

Caitlin retreated to her office, sat down at her desk and slipped off her shoes, careful to line them up just so, before glancing at the entry that had her assistant in a tailspin.

Not that she blamed her. In the five years since IMAGEine, Caitlin's Minneapolis-based image consulting business, had teamed up with *Twin City Trends* for their annual makeover contest, this was the first time they'd received an entry from a man.

She deliberately turned the photograph over to escape the intensity of those deep-set, charcoal-gray eyes.

"Now, Mr...." Caitlin glanced at the name at the top of the entry form. "Walsh. What's your story?"

She turned the application over to skim the "in one hundred words or less tell us why you need a makeover" portion of the entry form and was surprised to find it handwritten rather than typed. And even more surprised to see the neat penmanship dominated by carefully rounded letters; the lower case ones graced with decorative, curly tails.

Okay....

Caitlin lightly cleared her throat.

As she skimmed the essay, unexpected emotion grabbed

hold of her heart. And squeezed. No wonder Sabrina hadn't known what to do with this particular entry.

She didn't know what to do with it, either.

And Caitlin always knew what to do about everything.

"Are you kidding me, Caitlin? You can't disqualify this entry. It's our winner!" Dawn Gallagher picked up the entry form and read the opening lines of the essay out loud.

"'Dear *Twin City Trends* Makeover Team,
My name is Jennifer Walsh. I'm twelve years old, and I'm writing to you because my dad needs a makeover…'"

"This is pure gold. Gold that happens to have a high rate of exchange at the newsstand."

"A person has to be eighteen or older to enter," Caitlin reminded her, wishing she'd followed her first instinct and quietly discarded Jennifer Walsh's entry form instead of showing it to Dawn. Blame it on the fact that she'd been charmed by the sweet formality of the girl's essay and thought Dawn might be, too. She'd had no idea the style editor would insist they'd found their winning entry.

"He is over eighteen," Dawn argued.

"But *he* didn't enter the contest."

"An insignificant detail."

"There is no such thing as an insignificant detail," Caitlin felt the need to point out.

Dawn stared at her for a moment and then dropped into the leather chair opposite Caitlin's desk. Caitlin waited, knowing from past experience that Dawn wasn't admitting defeat. She was plotting her next move.

"My senior editor posted the stats on the last issue, and I have to admit they're pretty dismal." Dawn's smile was strained. "Subscription sales have declined ever since our competition decided to publish a cheaper version of the magazine. Jillian is hoping the annual makeover edition will turn things around. In fact, she's hinted if that happens, she'll think about making the contest a monthly feature."

"With you in charge."

"Possibly." Dawn shrugged but couldn't hide the ambitious gleam in her eyes. "But might I remind you, if there's no increase in sales, there's no makeover feature. And if there's no makeover feature, there's no need for a style editor."

"I see your dilemma," Caitlin said dryly.

"You can't deny how much buzz this could create," Dawn continued. "A man featured in our contest. The entry sent in by his twelve-year-old daughter. It's fresh. It's intriguing."

"It has…potential."

Dawn's eyes sparkled. "And you have to admit, this guy…Devon Walsh…is mega-handsome. A diamond in the rough."

Caitlin frowned. A diamond in the rough? Had she missed something?

"You see it, don't you?" Dawn held up the photo. "He looks like an aging rock star. Silky dark hair. Mysterious eyes. Bad-boy stubble…"

Bad-boy stubble? Oh, please.

She'd definitely missed something.

"…unless you aren't sure you could improve on this." Dawn shrugged.

"Believe me, a shave would be an improvement," Caitlin shot back, aware of her friend's tactics but still a little offended that Dawn would question her ability.

"You've been hoping to increase your male clientele for the past few years. Who knows? If you can transform this partic-ular frog into a prince, execs will be lining up around the block to schedule an appointment at IMAGEine."

Caitlin thought the frog/prince analogy wasn't exactly a fair one. Devon Walsh might be on the scruffy side but he did have great cheekbones. And she couldn't deny that one of her goals included expanding her client base to include more men. Still, she couldn't help but wonder if the whole thing wasn't a setup.

"Are you sure about this? For all we know, Devon Walsh is a wannabe actor or model who put his daughter up to this, knowing we'd take the bait."

Hook, line and show-me-the-rise-in-subscriptions sinker.

"Your cynicism is showing, my friend, but if it makes you feel better, pay Jennifer Walsh and her dad a visit to make sure this is legit before we sign on the dotted line. If it isn't, we'll go with *your* top pick. Plain and simple."

Plain and simple.

It sounded good in theory. So why did Caitlin have the uneasy feeling that her life was about to get complicated?

Just before lunch, Devon Walsh noticed that an eerie silence had descended over the house.

An eerie silence could only mean one thing. His children were studying instead of playing.

He pushed his chair away from the desk and stalked toward the door as he formulated a slight variation of the lecture he'd been serving up like spaghetti over the past few months. A lecture he'd guarantee couldn't be found in one of the numerous parenting books he'd been reading. The ones that gave advice on how to give children roots, wings and make them mind without losing his.

Devon was beginning to think the reason he hadn't discovered a fool-proof parenting technique was because his children didn't exactly fit the typical "kid" mold....

Sure, blame them. It's not like you're the poster child for Father of the Year....

Not that he wasn't trying.

It's just that three out of the four Walshes in the house weren't cooperating.

He decided to track down Josh and Brady, his nine-year-old twins, first. Just the fact there were two of them doubled the volume and usually made them easier to locate. Jenny was the tough one. Shy and introspective, she could make herself practically invisible when she wanted to be. And she wanted to be. A lot.

Coaxing Jenny out of her shell was a challenge Devon didn't feel prepared for.

Who was he kidding? *Parenting* was a challenge he didn't feel prepared for.

Strength for the moment, right, Lord?

It had become his mantra over the past six months.

"Brady? Josh?" Devon veered to the right when he reached the foot of the stairs, assuming he'd find the boys in the parlor— a quaint, old-fashioned term for a drafty room with scuffed hardwood floors, uncomfortable furniture covered in itchy, burgundy velvet and heavy drapes that blocked out the light with the efficiency of an eclipse. For reasons Devon couldn't begin to explain, it had become his children's favorite room in the house.

He'd only taken a few steps in that direction when the twins materialized in front of him.

"Hi, Dad," Josh said cheerfully.

Too cheerfully, in Devon's opinion. And even if the chapter on "pushing boundaries" he'd read the night before wasn't still fresh in his mind, he would have been suspicious.

Brady pulled his ever-present stopwatch out of his pants pocket and flipped open the cover. "You've got thirty-five minutes left to write, Dad. What's up?"

"I was just about to ask you the same thing."

"Ah…nothing much. Just hanging around." Josh casually tossed a miniature football into the air and scrambled to catch it again. He missed and it bounced off his shoe and hit the wall. "Playing football. You know."

Devon's eyes narrowed. The boys had never shown an interest in any of the sports equipment he'd purchased. A decoy toy, no doubt about it.

"Where is Jenny?" Devon took a step toward the parlor and found his path blocked by identical brown-eyed obstacles.

"She's...somewhere." Brady shrugged.

"Not here, though." Josh's ears turned red.

Devon suppressed a smile. Those ears gave him away every time. More reliable than a lie-detector test.

"Is she in the parlor?"

"No!" The twins' voices blended together in an ear-splitting, off-key soprano.

Devon winced. He wasn't in any hurry for the boys to grow up but he did look forward to the day their voices changed.

"Will you help us put together the train track, Dad?" Brady asked.

"You want to put together the train track?" Devon repeated. *"Now?"*

The twins nodded vigorously.

"Yeah."

"We want to get started."

"Let me get this straight. You're talking about the model train that's been sitting in the box since I brought it home? *A month ago?"*

Josh and Brady exchanged is-this-a-trick question frowns and then reverted to the silent mode of communication that had unnerved Devon when they'd first moved in with him. It had taken Jenny to put it in perspective.

"It's a twin thing, Dad," she'd said. *"It's like trying to figure out how peanut butter gets on the ceiling."*

And because the whole peanut-butter phenomenon was

another unsolved mystery in his household, Devon took his daughter's advice to accept what he couldn't explain and move on. It was easier—and maybe a little safer—that way.

"We were waiting for the right moment." Brady, official timekeeper for the Walsh family, grinned at him.

If it weren't for Josh's ears, now a deep shade of crimson, Devon might have fallen for it.

He decided right then and there to get a refund on every single parenting book stacked up next to his bed. Or maybe he should just chuck his next mystery novel and write a parenting book instead. At least it wouldn't take long. He could probably finish the entire five pages in an hour.

The door leading to the parlor flew open and Jenny appeared.

"Is she here yet…?" A tiny squeak replaced the rest of the sentence when the girl spotted her father standing in the hallway.

Devon frowned. "Is who here yet?"

"Dad!" Jenny gulped. "What are you doing down here? It isn't break time for—"

"Thirty-one minutes," Brady supplied helpfully.

Devon's gaze zeroed in on his daughter. "Did I miss something? Are we expecting company this morning?"

"N-no."

"I'm not expecting company," Josh interjected. "Are you expecting company, Brady?"

"I'm not expecting company—"

Devon's head started to swim and he held up his hand. "Now that we've established the fact *none of us* is expecting company, maybe we should all go into the kitchen and rustle up something for—"

The doorbell interrupted him and Devon's eyebrows shot up.

"Mmm. I wonder who that could be." He took a step forward and all three children attached themselves to him like ticks on a deer.

"It's probably the mailman," Jenny said. "I'll get it."

"Yeah, Dad. You go upstairs and write. You still have…" It wasn't easy but Brady managed to wrestle his stopwatch out of his pocket again *and* keep a death grip on his father. "Twenty-eight minutes until lunch."

"Oh, this is much more interesting than lunch—"

A piercing shriek interrupted him, cutting through the last mournful notes of the doorbell.

Devon closed his eyes. "Josh, did you put Sunny back in her cage after breakfast?"

There was one long, supercharged moment of silence.

"No."

"I didn't think so."

His children still clinging to him, Devon strode toward the door to revive whoever was on the other side. Because the way the morning continued to unravel, the poor woman—and the shriek had definitely been feminine—had probably fallen over in a dead faint.

Devon yanked the door open, ignoring the loud protests of his soon-to-be-grounded-for-life children—because according to the books, grounding was a perfectly acceptable form of discipline—and braced himself to find an unconscious woman sprawled across the welcome mat.

It was a woman, all right.

A very attractive, very *conscious* woman. Classic features. Glossy dark hair with a faint mahogany sheen. Eyes the same shade of blue as his favorite pair of jeans.

She was standing on the porch wearing a stylish black suit paired with ridiculously high heels.

And was holding Josh's iguana in her arms.

Chapter Two

It was a good thing, Caitlin thought, *that her youngest sister taught middle-school science.* Because it meant Evie always had a veritable zoo of creatures living in her classroom—creatures she insisted Caitlin learn to appreciate by getting up close and personal with them when she visited.

If not for the benefit of that prior *Wild Kingdom* education, the sight of the two-foot-long lizard, curled up on the enclosed sun porch next to a sleeping dachshund of roughly the same size, might have really freaked her out.

As it was, the reptile had managed to wring a brief but embarrassing scream out of her. But that was only because the moment she'd dismissed the motionless creature as a realistic chew toy made out of some high-tech scaly fiber, it had come to life and barreled toward her as if she were a long-lost cousin. Apparently not caring that the closest kinship Caitlin could claim to a member of his species was the faux alligator-skin bag hanging in her closet.

Not sure of the creature's intent but knowing that one assertive move deserved another, Caitlin had bent down and simply picked it up. The lizard then draped itself comfortably over her arm and proceeded to study the gold and sapphire earring dangling from her ear.

As she contemplated the odds of those intimidating claws *not* doing irreparable damage to her silk blouse, the front door opened. Judging from the expressions on the faces of the people crowded together in the doorway, she now had the honor of being the strangest creature on the porch.

One of the little boys, a mirror image of the other, darted forward, flashed a smile more mischievous than apologetic, and took the iguana from her.

Officially making it five—no, make that six because she probably should include the dachshund—against one.

Caitlin turned her attention to Devon Walsh—not only the tallest one in the group but instantly recognizable by his bad-boy stubble—and felt her heart skip a beat.

The photo hadn't done him justice.

Oh, his hair *was* on the shaggy side, and he obviously wasn't in a committed relationship with a razor. But she'd only noticed the brooding eyes and had somehow missed the lines fanning out on either side of them. Intriguing pleats that looked ready to capture the fall-out from his next smile.

Too bad she wasn't going to witness that smile. Because at the moment he was scowling at her as if she were trespassing on private property.

Maybe because you are? She thought.

Not exactly true, so Caitlin ignored the pesky voice. After all, Devon Walsh *was* expecting her. And she hadn't seen any No Trespassing signs posted, although the formidable iron-scrolled gate surrounding the perimeter of the Walsh's yard had given her pause. For that matter, so had the house itself. The gloomy Gothic-style Victorian, sporting a coat of blistered gunmetal-gray paint and cloaked in ivy, resembled an abandoned Hollywood movie set more than a home. It looked as out of place in the tidy row of well-kept homes as an ordinary rock tossed into a jewelry box.

Caitlin took a careful breath but before she could say a word, Devon Walsh stepped forward and propped his hands on his lean hips, effectively blocking the children from view.

Caitlin had the strangest feeling that that was his intent.

"Can I help you?" The question was polite even though his tone implied it was the last thing he wanted to do.

"I'm Caitlin McBride. I have an appointment with you this morning and—"

"I don't think so."

Caitlin blinked at the terse interruption but then decided to ignore it. "I left a message yesterday, and your secretary called me back to set up our meeting."

Devon shook his head. "That's a new one. You're a lawyer, right? Vickie sent you."

"A lawyer? No." Caitlin gave a choke of disbelief and glanced down at the outfit she'd chosen that morning. Not that she expected a man who wore a ratty tweed sweater with *suede elbow patches* to understand that a female attorney wouldn't pair a multicolored chain-link belt with a conservative business suit. The only reason she could get away with it was because she *pretended* that it worked. Which, in turn, made it work. Confidence. It was her favorite accessory. "I'm an image consultant. I explained that on the phone."

If anything, he looked even more skeptical. "So you go door-to-door, selling makeup?"

Caitlin bristled. She didn't know what kind of game Devon Walsh was playing, or why he was pretending to be ignorant about their appointment, but she knew one thing. The guy needed a personality makeover more than a haircut.

"No. I. Do. Not." Caitlin forced the words out through gritted teeth. *"Our meeting,"* she emphasized the words to jog his memory, "was to discuss the essay Jennifer wrote for the contest."

The girl peeking out from behind Devon Walsh's long, denim-clad leg let out a tiny gasp but her father didn't seem to notice. Nor did he notice his children—all three of them—suddenly pull a disappearing act that would have made Houdini envious.

Even the dachshund vanished through the doggy door.

The wariness in Devon's eyes turned to confusion. "Contest?"

"The makeover contest for *Twin City Trends* magazine."

"Let me get this straight. Are you telling me that Jenny entered a makeover contest?"

"No—"

"Well, that's a relief."

"She entered *you*."

Devon heard three words—*Twin City Trends*—and suddenly found himself wishing that Caitlin McBride *was* a lawyer. Because magazines meant reporters…and reporters meant publicity. And publicity? Well, that was something he'd successfully managed to avoid. Until now.

But if Caitlin McBride was telling the truth, somehow his daughter—his serious, sweet, painfully shy daughter—had brought it right to their front door.

The question was, why?

"Would I be correct in assuming you didn't know anything about the contest, Mr. Walsh?" Caitlin's question tugged Devon back to reality. And scraped against his senses. Somehow her husky, bluesy voice didn't match up with the stylish clothes and cool demeanor.

Devon didn't let himself dwell on the intriguing contradiction. Not when his relationship with Caitlin McBride was only destined to last another fifteen or twenty seconds. Tops.

"Oh, you'd definitely be correct about that."

"And that you don't have a secretary?"

"Two for two, Ms. McBride. I'm sorry you wasted your time coming here this morning. And now if you'll excuse me, I'm going to get to the bottom of this." Devon forced a polite smile, started to close the door and suddenly discovered Caitlin McBride standing next to him in the foyer.

"Good idea." She smiled up at him. "I'm a little curious myself."

Devon blinked, wondering if he could blame his momentary lapse in homeland security on the scent of Caitlin's perfume—a rich blend of exotic spices that definitely packed a punch to the senses. Or maybe it was her smile. The one that warmed up the indigo eyes like sunlight on water.

Get a grip, Walsh. Somehow she's involved with the media.

"No offense, Ms. McBride, but this is a family matter."

"A family matter I received a personal invitation to when Jennifer entered you in the makeover contest."

Makeover contest.

Devon winced at the reminder while silently scrolling through his options. If he told Caitlin to leave, it was possible she'd turn up again with reinforcements. That had been his brief but memorable experience with the press in the past. She might claim to be an "image consultant" but it didn't mean she wasn't employed by the magazine. Or that a single headline wouldn't disrupt his life. Again.

Keep your friends close and your enemies closer. Devon decided to take the old adage to heart. And because he couldn't figure out which category Caitlin McBride belonged in, he decided to let her stay.

All he had to do was get Jenny to admit she'd entered him in the contest as a practical joke and Caitlin would be on her way. To find another victim.

"Roundtable meeting, Jenny," Devon bellowed as he passed the staircase. "Parlor. Five minutes."

He strode down the hall, surprised that Caitlin managed to match him step for step in shoes jacked up by pencil-thin heels. And even though she stared straight ahead, Devon had the strangest feeling she was taking in everything around her.

Great.

Devon was well aware the house had its shortcomings, but he still considered it an answer to prayer. Proof that God wasn't silent and far away but close and listening. And real. That the ramshackle Victorian needed a lot of work hadn't bothered him. And even though it would have sounded strange if he tried to put words to it, from the moment Devon had glimpsed the For Sale sign in the knee-high grass behind the fence, he'd felt an immediate kinship with the house.

After he'd signed the papers and accepted the overwhelming task of remodeling it room by room, the project had done more than fill long hours. It had started the healing process.

Not something the average visitor would understand or even appreciate. And he wasn't going to apologize for the multitude of little things that still needed attention...

Devon sent Rosie's rawhide bone spinning out of the way with a discreet kick and then noticed the innocent-looking cardboard box positioned against the wall just outside the parlor door.

His lips twitched. Subtle, the twins weren't. Thank goodness.

Lately, they'd started to act out scenes from the book he'd been reading to them after supper. A book that happened to be an action-adventure novel—loaded with peril and cool gadgets—about Matt and Marty Ransom, teenage brothers on a quest to find their missing father while staying one step ahead of the resident villain.

Without even auditioning for the part, Devon had been drafted into their reenactments and cast in the role of evil Dr. Chamberlain. Over the past two days, he'd found a miniature tape recorder hidden in his medicine cabinet and the bedroom doorknob dusted with something Devon guessed was a homemade version of "fingerprint" powder. He even stumbled into an ingenious trap made out of paper cups and shaving cream.

Devon was thrilled. For two boys whose lives had been scheduled down to the last second of the day, their imaginative play over the past few weeks had been a major breakthrough.

Not that he could begin to explain all that to the woman walking beside him. He slanted a glance at Caitlin McBride and saw her lips flatline as she stepped delicately over the misshapen bedroom slipper that Sunny and her favorite partner in crime, Rosie had been wrestling over that morning.

No, Caitlin McBride wouldn't understand. And because he doubted she'd find a shaving-cream bomb humorous, he paused before approaching the box.

"Wait here for a second."

Caitlin blinked. "You're kidding me, right?"

Apparently not. Because instead of answering her question, Devon sidled up to an ordinary cardboard box as cautiously as a bomb-squad tech. Caitlin's back teeth ground together. She was convinced the man was deliberately trying to drive her crazy in an attempt to get her to leave.

Not that it wasn't tempting. But she'd made the decision to stick around a split second after Devon had smiled politely and tried to shut the door in her face. And only one thing had prevented her from admitting defeat and calling the runner-up in the contest.

Jenny.

When the girl had peeked around her father, Caitlin had had a flashback of herself at the tender age of twelve. Confused. Hopeful. Scared. A bundle of conflicting emotions reflected in that pair of large copper-brown eyes.

My mom is gone and my Dad needs some advice on clothes. He thinks he looks okay but he could use some help from a professional....

The rest of Jennifer's earnest essay had replayed in Caitlin's mind. She couldn't deny that Jennifer's father did need both help *and* advice but she had a feeling he wasn't the type of person who would accept it graciously.

And that's why she'd decided to stay. Because whatever Jennifer's reasons were for sending in that contest entry, Caitlin was going to make certain the girl wasn't punished for it.

Devon picked up a piece of hose hanging out of the side of the box and spoke into it. "I'll be back in a few minutes to put this box out with the recyclables."

Caitlin held back a smile as his words raised a duet of muffled protests from inside the box. Devon ignored them and motioned for her to follow him. When they reached the end of the narrow hall, he stood to the side.

"It should be safe in here."

The warmth of the room surprised Caitlin. Granted, the old-fashioned parlor, painted a soft, seashell-pink and trimmed with oak crown moldings, needed a serious update but there was a certain "shabby chic" charm to the brushed-velvet furniture and hand-hooked wool rugs scattered on the hardwood floor.

A round coffee table anchored the center of the room like the hub of a wheel with four colorful, oversized pillows arranged like spokes around it.

While Caitlin silently worked out the challenge those pillows presented to a knee-length skirt without a kick pleat, Jenny slipped into the room.

Now that the girl wasn't hiding behind her dad, Caitlin had a chance to study her more closely. Already tall for her age, Jennifer Walsh's final growth spurt would put her at a willowy five foot nine or ten inches. At the moment, though, she was all arms and legs and awkward motion.

Jenny's hair, as dark as her father's and with a natural wave she probably hadn't learned to appreciate yet, was subdued in a long ponytail. The wire-frame glasses that had slipped halfway down her nose magnified the unusual color of her eyes.

Eyes that widened in panic when they met Caitlin's.

Caitlin gave her what she hoped was a reassuring smile and perched on the edge of a Windsor chair next to the sofa.

"Take a seat." Devon motioned to a pillow and Jenny hesitated. The uncertainty on the girl's face made Caitlin's mouth dry up.

Was she afraid of her father?

Parent and child stared at each other across the table and Caitlin discreetly fished around in her purse until her fingers closed around her cell phone. Just in case.

Devon crossed his arms. "Okay, Jenny—you've got some 'splainin' to do."

Caitlin sucked in a breath. Devon's voice had changed. But it wasn't angry or threatening. It sounded suspiciously like an impersonation of Ricky Ricardo from an episode of *I Love Lucy*.

Jenny giggled.

Devon gave his daughter a teasing wink and a smile.

And Caitlin forgot how to breathe.

Because the wink erased any remaining signs of a scowl. And the tender smile he aimed at Jenny…

Dawn had been right. Devon Walsh's smile alone would launch a thousand subscriptions.

He reached out and tweaked the girl's foot. "Now, why don't you tell me what's going on so we can get on with our day and Ms. McBride can get back to work?"

"I entered you in a…makeover contest I heard about on the radio last week," Jenny admitted.

"As a joke, right? Did the boys put you up to it?"

"No!"

Devon frowned. "You think I need a…makeover?"

Jenny looked at Caitlin, who nodded imperceptibly. Yes, *tact* was the key word here.

"You…I, um…"

Caitlin came to her rescue. "Would you like me to show your dad the essay you wrote?"

The girl didn't say so out loud, but the relief mirrored in her eyes had Caitlin reaching into her purse once again. She handed Devon the entry form.

Devon scanned the short paragraph on the back and if anything, he looked more confused than before.

"Professional help," he muttered and glanced up at Caitlin.

She inclined her head in answer to the unspoken question.

Yes, that would be me. The professional.

"I don't understand, Jenny." Devon plowed his fingers through his hair. "Why didn't you talk to me about this first?"

Jenny twisted her fingers together in her lap. "I heard you talking on the phone to Aunt Vickie," she finally said in a low voice. "She wants to take you to court to get us back—"

"*Jenny!*" Devon's gaze cut to Caitlin as his daughter rushed on.

"And she called you a…bum. I thought if you won the contest, the magazine people could help you look good in front of the judge. Then we'd be able to stay with you."

Chapter Three

A dozen thoughts crashed over Devon at once, immobilizing him.

Jenny had overheard his recent phone conversation with her aunt, Vickie Heath. And even though Jenny hadn't heard both sides, somehow she'd guessed the woman's intentions correctly. Which probably had something to due with the fact that Vickie had shown up at the airport to confront Devon the day he'd arrived to take his children home.

Not caring that her niece and nephews were huddled together within earshot, Vickie had claimed he was an unfit parent. A selfish recluse who planned to deny Jenny and her brothers the life of privilege and opportunity that Ashleigh, their mother, had wanted them to have.

If Devon remembered correctly, Vickie had also thrown the words *worthless bum* into the mix.

Until Vickie's phone call, he'd assumed his former sister-in-law's tirade at the airport was simply a release of the stress and grief over Ashleigh's untimely death. Never in a million years had he dreamed that his ex-wife's sister planned to contest the placement of the children.

His children.

Somehow Jenny had gotten wind of Vickie's intentions and decided that if a judge had to choose a parent, it wasn't going to be the guy with unfashionably long hair and faded blue jeans who didn't appear to have a steady job.

Devon stifled a groan. By bringing Caitlin McBride, an image consultant who had a professional relationship with *Twin City Trends,* to their door, Jenny had complicated the situation instead of helping it. All it would take was a few careless words from Jenny or the boys and he'd have reporters camped out on the sidewalk.

Devon wasn't about to sign his family up for that three-ring circus again.

Lord, it took so long to get the kids back. To be a family. I don't want to lose them now.

Even as Devon sent up the silent appeal, he couldn't think of one thing to say to Jenny that wouldn't allow Caitlin further access to their family business. It was bad enough she'd heard the reason that prompted Jenny's contest entry; there was no telling what Caitlin would do if she knew the rest of the story.

Their eyes caught and held over Jenny's head.

It was time to show the lady the door. Again.

"Ms. McBride—"

She didn't let him finish.

"One of the contest rules is that the person chosen for the makeover must be over eighteen. But because of Jenny's well-written essay we made an exception," Caitlin interrupted, aiming a warm smile in his daughter's direction. "I stopped by today to congratulate you, Jenny, and let you know your entry took second place. My assistant will be sending you a gift certificate for a style analysis from IMAGEine."

Devon gaped at Caitlin as she rose to her feet and held out her hand. To his daughter.

"Congratulations. It was nice to meet you, Jenny. And you, Mr. Walsh."

Automatically, Devon followed her lead and extended his hand, too. After a slight hesitation, Caitlin pressed her fingers against his. He expected her touch to be as cool as her eyes, but instead the brief touch sparked a current that jump-started a part of his heart he'd thought lay dormant.

Maybe that was the part of the reason Devon didn't realize the truth until later on in the day, when he replayed the unusual conversation that had taken place in the parlor.

Caitlin McBride wouldn't have bothered to set up an appointment to meet with them if Jenny had come in second place. They would have received a polite letter of congratulations, accompanied by the gift certificate she'd mentioned, and that would have been the end of it.

Jenny *had* won the contest.

But for some mysterious reason, Caitlin had walked away.

"You have a warm skin tone, so that means you want to choose clothing from this color palette." Caitlin spread some swatches out on the table for her client to look at. "Something on the order of this gold satin would be perfect for the dress you've been looking for to wear to your anniversary party."

"I don't know." Maxine Butterfield fidgeted with the enormous jade elephant dangling from a gold chain around her neck. "What about pink? People always compliment me when I wear pink."

Caitlin resisted the urge to demand names and phone numbers. "I'll drape a piece of this fabric around your shoulders and you'll see what I'm talking about."

Out of the corner of her eye, Caitlin saw the light on the telephone blink out a rapid SOS from Sabrina Buckley.

"Excuse me a moment, Mrs. Butterfield."

Maxine smiled and immediately reached for a swatch of pink suede as Caitlin walked back to her desk.

"Sabrina, I'm with a client right now so—"

"He's here." Sabrina cut her off with an excited whisper.

"Who's here?"

"Him."

"You have to be a little more specific."

"Him. Mr. Makeover. From the contest. You know…the guy you said has awesome cheekbones. Devon Walsh."

"He's in the office?" *Standing next to your desk? Listening to every word you just said about awesome cheekbones?*

And it wasn't even Monday.

"He wants to see you."

Caitlin's heart skipped a beat. Over the past week, she'd tried to put the whole episode with the Walsh family out of her mind. It hadn't been easy. Because for some odd reason, in the rare moments when Caitlin's thoughts weren't focused on her clients, they kept returning to Devon Walsh like a compass needle irresistibly drawn to the north. And she couldn't forget the stricken expression on his face when Jenny told him why she'd entered him in the contest.

We'll be able to stay with you.

Caitlin firmly pushed the memory aside. IMAGEine was her business, she reminded herself, *not* the Walsh family.

"He just poured himself a cup of coffee." Sabrina kept up a whispered play-by-play. "Now he's looking at the before-and-after photos on the wall."

And he can still hear every word you're saying.

"Tell Mr. Walsh that I'm booked solid for the next three weeks but if you check my calendar, you might be able to pencil him in after the etiquette class a week from Wednesday."

"He said he doesn't need an appointment."

Caitlin blinked, momentarily caught off guard. Of all the

nerve. Only her immediate family, consisting of her father and her sisters, Evie and Meghan, had permission to bypass standard office protocol.

"Everyone needs an appointment."

"He said he doesn't need an appointment because he has a gift certificate."

A gift certificate.

The one she'd asked Sabrina to drop in the mail the day after she'd been at the Walsh's. The one she'd promptly forgotten about because she assumed it would end up lining the bottom of an iguana cage.

"Is this a chocolate factory, Sabrina?"

"Ah…" Sabrina hesitated a fraction of a second. "No?"

"So a gift certificate from IMAGEine isn't the equivalent of a golden ticket from Willy Wonka, is it?"

"Are you talking about the original or the remake? Because I heard there were some differences, and I saw the one with Johnny Depp but missed the first one with that other guy so I'm not sure—"

"*Sabrina.*"

"Right. He needs an appointment. But he—"

Caitlin heard Maxine laugh gleefully as she unearthed a bright raspberry, chiffon swatch from the summer color palette. "Just a second, Sabrina. Mrs. Butterfield…look at that attractive pumpkin-and-black houndstooth check."

Maxine's double chin wobbled, warning Caitlin she'd already lost ground.

"He says he doesn't mind waiting," Sabrina rushed on.

"Fine. I'll be done in an hour. If Mr. Walsh doesn't want to set up an appointment, I can spare five minutes after that."

"Oh." Sabrina's upbeat tone deflated like a balloon animal in a room full of preschool children.

"Is something wrong?"

"It's just that I have a date for dinner tonight, remember? If you add in rush-hour traffic, a shower and twenty minutes to fix my hair, I'll be late. And you always stress how important it is to be punctual...." Sabrina's voice trailed off into a hopeful silence.

Caitlin suppressed a smile. Hoisted with her own petard. "I'll close up tonight."

On time, Caitlin thought as she hung up the phone. She was confident Devon would view an hour spent in the reception area, with nothing to read but fashion magazines, with the same enthusiasm he'd have while waiting in a dentist's office for a root canal.

The longer Devon waited for Caitlin to make an appearance the more he questioned his sanity.

If the glossy style magazines artfully fanned out on chrome-and-glass-topped tables hadn't convinced him that he didn't belong there, the wall of pictures featuring IMAGEine's clients should have sent him running from the building. The photos provided all the proof he needed that Caitlin's entire business centered around the warped philosophy that the only thing that really mattered was what a person looked like on the outside.

Because a First Impression Lasts...

The words, stenciled in gold letters below the IMAGEine logo on the wall, made Devon wonder why Caitlin hadn't put her business's tagline around a full-length mirror.

If it hadn't been for Jenny, he wouldn't be here at all.

Unfortunately, it had been his daughter's turn to pick up the mail the day the letter arrived with IMAGEine's return address stamped in the corner.

Jenny had immediately tracked him down and extracted the gift certificate with an enthusiasm Devon hadn't seen since she and the boys had moved in with him. But when Devon had hemmed and hawed about actually exchanging the gift certificate for a free style analysis—whatever that was—Jenny's copper-brown eyes had darkened with concern.

"You have to use it, Dad. You're the one who's over eighteen. Ms. McBride's feelings will get hurt if you don't."

And because he cared about his *daughter's* feelings, he'd given in. Jenny didn't have to know that he planned to give Ms. McBride the gift certificate back and suggest she give it to someone else.

Someone who *needed* it.

"Mr. Walsh?"

Devon looked at Sabrina Buckley, wondering if Caitlin's assistant ever spoke above a whisper. Studies did prove that a stressful work environment took a toll on a person.

"It's two minutes to five. I have a date tonight and it takes twenty minutes to straighten my hair with a flat iron so I'm going to scoot out now."

Whatever a flat iron was, it didn't sound like something that should be used in the same sentence as *hair*. But what did he know?

"Have fun."

Sabrina flashed a charming smile as she gathered up her things. When she reached the door, she paused and looked back. "It's a shame you're too busy to be in our makeover contest, Mr. Walsh. You do have really great cheekbones."

"Thanks." *I think.*

The young woman slipped out of the office, and Devon tilted his head thoughtfully.

It's a shame you're too busy to be in our makeover contest.

So that was the spin Caitlin had put on the situation. And it affirmed that his original suspicion had been right. For some inexplicable reason, she *had* let him off the hook.

When the door behind the reception area opened a few minutes later an elderly woman, dressed from head to toe in lavender, emerged and made a beeline for the exit. Muttering something about swatches and pumpkins.

She spotted Devon and pointed her finger at him. "Don't let her push you around," she muttered. "*Everybody* looks good in pink."

Devon closed his eyes.

Tell me why I'm here, Lord?

When he opened them again, the first thing Devon saw was Caitlin. She swept into the room with the easy, unaffected grace of a ballet dancer. Clutching both of her shoes in one perfectly manicured hand while she tugged her hair free from a gold clip with the other.

Devon grinned.

She needed to change her logo. First impressions *didn't* always last.

Chapter Four

She had to be dreaming.

Or hallucinating.

Those were the only explanations Caitlin could come up with when she saw Devon Walsh in a casual slouch next to the coffee station, his lean frame and tousled dark hair a striking contrast against the ivory and apricot wallpaper.

Caitlin ignored the sudden, erratic thumping of her heart and let her professional instincts kick into gear.

With a practiced eye, her assessment began at the scuffed loafers on Devon's feet and went from there. Jeans so faded they looked more white than blue. The loose, uneven hem of his black fisherman's sweater proved he hadn't followed the proper washing instructions on the label: Hand Wash, Dry Flat. He'd pushed the sleeves up to his elbows, revealing corded forearms still tanned a golden brown from the summer sun.

But somehow, dark-eyed, unshaven and slightly rumpled, Devon Walsh still managed to spark the strangest feeling that he was the type of man a woman would run *to* for protection, not away from.

And if that unwelcome thought hadn't been enough to throw

off Caitlin's balance, the slow smile Devon aimed in her direction momentarily stripped away her ability to speak.

Because that was the moment Caitlin remembered her shoes. The shoes she'd taken off on her way down the hall. The shoes she now held in her hand.

She'd had enough moments of acute embarrassment early on in her life to know that the floor, no matter how much one wished it, *never* opened up and swallowed a person whole, saving one from complete and utter mortification.

One had to save oneself. And one saved oneself by appearing confident and self-assured no matter what the circumstances.

Caitlin lifted her chin and met his gaze without flinching, resisting the urge to smooth back the strands of hair that had flopped over one eye when she'd pulled out the hair clip. "Good afternoon, Mr. Walsh."

Responding to her tone, Devon's smile obediently subsided into a small but beguiling twitch at the corner of his lips. "Ms. McBride."

"You've been waiting a long time—" Caitlin's heart jumped in time with the unsettling thought that suddenly came to mind. Given Devon's guarded reception the first time they'd met, she could think of only one thing that might compel him to pace the floor of IMAGEine's reception area for nearly an hour.

Or one *person*.

Even though it was none of her business, Caitlin found herself asking anyway. "Is everything all right with Jennifer?"

Devon frowned. "Jenny's fine."

Caitlin decided the unexpected relief she felt was due to empathy—after all, she'd practically relived her own adolescence every time her eyes had met Jenny's—and not due to any…*maternal*…instincts.

Caitlin was fairly certain she didn't have any of those.

Other than the etiquette classes she taught twice a month,

her exposure to children was limited. She left the nurturing to her two younger sisters, who seemed to have a special knack for it. Evie and Meghan drew children in as effortlessly as the tinkling bells on the neighborhood ice-cream truck.

There were times Caitlin listened to her peers raise concerns about when to marry and start a family, but she'd never been inclined to join in the conversation. She paid more attention to her wristwatch than her biological clock. And it was difficult to hear the ticking of that particular clock over the voices of her clients.

Successful businesses didn't just happen. Someone had to *make* them happen. And in order to make them happen, a person had to be willing to make sacrifices. To keep her eyes trained on the goal and not get distracted by things that might take her *off* the goal...

The reminder brought Caitlin up short. She focused on a point just past Devon's shoulder and deliberately kept her tone brisk and businesslike.

"Well, if you aren't here about Jenny, Mr. Walsh, what can I do for you?"

Landing on her feet, Devon thought with admiration, *was obviously something Caitlin McBride had perfected.*

And it didn't even require shoes.

How much energy did it take to keep the slight edge honed on that husky contralto? To keep her features as smooth and ex-pressionless as a marble statue?

But Devon knew he'd glimpsed something...some flicker of indefinable emotion in her eyes when she'd asked about Jenny.

And it made him curious.

"The gift certificate. I..." *Came to return it.* That's what Devon had planned to say. But for some reason, the words that came out of his mouth didn't sound like that at all. In fact, they sounded more like "I have no clue what a style analysis is."

That Devon even remembered the term shocked him.

Caitlin appeared a little shocked, too.

Somehow, it made Devon feel better.

She crossed her arms and eyed him like a boxer sizing up an opponent on the other side of the ring. "What do you do for a living, Mr. Walsh?"

Devon frowned. "What does that have to do with anything?"

"Humor me."

Don't forget, you started this, Devon reminded himself with a sigh. "I'm a writer."

"A writer." Caitlin's straight little nose pleated like an accordion, the only evidence of her opinion about his chosen career. "But what do you do for a...*living?*"

"That's what I do."

Caitlin's eyebrows arched in doubt, giving Devon the impression that if his answers were earning points, his response had just plunged him into the negative digits.

"All right. And do you work out of your..." A delicate pause while she searched for the right word. "*Home*...or do you have an office?"

"My home."

"Interests?"

Keeping his family together immediately came to mind. But Devon wasn't about to open that door. Not even a crack.

"I do a little carpentry. Remodeling projects. Are you, ah, going somewhere with all this or did you forget the original question?"

Caitlin's lips twitched but Devon wasn't sure if she was trying to hide her irritation or subdue a smile.

"I didn't forget the question. These are some of the things I ask all my clients during the initial assessment. You see, everyone has a unique style based on a number of different things. Personality. Profession. Lifestyle. Hobbies. Together these form the image we present to others. I help people project their true—"

Devon stopped listening.

That's what it always came down to, he thought cynically. And it was all Ashleigh had cared about after her modeling career had taken off.

I can't let people know that I grew up in this little hick town. I have to wear designer clothes—that's what people expect. Devon, don't wear those old blue jeans when we go out. You are so stubborn. Can't you at least pretend to care that a photographer might be watching?

Devon had discovered that he couldn't. That world—the one that Ashleigh had enthusiastically embraced—seemed so *fake.* But because it had been important to his wife, Devon had supported her dreams. Until the day Ashleigh had demanded a divorce and he had to accept he was no longer part of them.

Devon didn't bother to hide his disgust. "Image. I don't care about that kind of thing."

Caitlin regarded him for a long moment. "And that is *exactly* the image you present, Mr. Walsh. That you don't care."

The quiet statement hit Devon with the force of a two-by-four and he stared at her in disbelief. "You're basing a lot on a pair of blue jeans and…" Devon glanced down to see what he'd fished out of the drawer that morning. "A sweater, Ms. McBride."

"It's not the clothes you're wearing—it's the chip on your shoulder that completes the ensemble. The one that might make a person, let's say a *judge* for instance, wonder what else you don't care about. Paying the bills? Making sure your children are fed? Safe? Well-adjusted?"

"Chip on my—" Wait a second. Ensemble? Men didn't have ensembles. Devon's back teeth ground together. "You are way out of line. You can't determine whether I'm a good parent by the label on my back pocket."

"You're right. I can't," Caitlin said simply. "But Jenny is obviously worried that *someone* will. And if I'm not mistaken, that's the reason she entered you in the makeover contest."

All the fight drained out of Devon at the sound of his daughter's name. And at the realization that he'd been more concerned about the press discovering his children's whereabouts than he had been about the reason Jenny had sent in the entry form in the first place.

Devon scraped his fingers through his hair and then wondered how it had gotten so long. He'd had it cut in...

Six months ago.

Devon stifled a groan. How had the time gotten away from him?

He knew how. Because over the past six months he'd poured his heart and soul into rebuilding his family.

If he lacked a social life it was because he preferred it that way. His brief but memorable experience with the media had forced him from his hometown to a city large enough to allow him to fade into the background.

Unlike Ashleigh, Devon avoided the limelight. An eccentricity his publisher assumed he'd eventually overcome.

Devon knew better.

Since Jenny and the boys arrived, he'd been forced to widen the narrow boundaries of his social circle—what remained of it anyway—to include the small congregation of New Hope Fellowship.

Devon had started attending the church after moving to Minneapolis. He acknowledged the importance of meeting with other believers, but he'd still managed to keep the people there at arm's length.

He knew the sudden appearance of his children would raise questions, but when Pastor Albright found out their mother had recently passed away, kindness trumped the natural curiosity their presence created in the congregation. After a gentle, collective offer to "let them know if they could help," people maintained a respectful distance.

And even though Devon had appreciated the friendly smiles and genuine concern, he'd been careful not to need any help.

Because what he needed the most was time. Time for him and the children to get to know each other. Time to collect every piece of information—no matter how small or seemingly insignificant—and piece it together to form a picture of the lives they'd lived while they'd been apart from him.

And even though Devon tried to convince himself that another judge wouldn't separate them, he'd thought the same thing at the first custody hearing. The one Ashleigh hadn't even bothered to attend. She'd sent her attorney instead, who'd dissected Devon's life and displayed it to the court. And made it look as if he were the last person capable of raising three small children.

Maybe it *was* time to ask for help.

Devon's first impulse was to reject the thought. Okay, his hair did need a trim. And he *could* use a trip to the men's department for some new clothes. But that didn't mean he needed help from a professional image consultant....

Did he?

A verse suddenly filtered through Devon's mind, as if in response to his silent question.

Man looks at the outward appearance, but the Lord looks at the heart.

Devon winced, knowing he couldn't argue with that. And like it or not, it backed up Caitlin's business logo. Now the question came down to whether or not he was going to swallow his pride and take advantage of her expertise.

And the gift certificate.

Devon hooked his thumbs in the back pockets of his jeans as he silently scrolled through his options. And tried to ignore the one standing right in front of him.

For the first time, Devon pondered—very briefly—the timing of their meeting. It occurred to him that his tendency to avoid civilization was working against him at the moment. When it came down to it, he didn't know many people....

But Caitlin McBride, Lord? You've got to be kidding me, right?

The woman was wound way too tight. Not to mention that she'd be impossible to work with. Devon had no doubt she could straighten up a platoon of soldiers simply by lifting one perfectly arched eyebrow.

Devon's gaze shifted and he caught Caitlin in the act of surreptitiously blowing a few wayward strands of hair out of her eyes.

It seemed that every time Devon thought he'd figured her out, he caught an intriguing glimpse of another side of her personality. A *softer* side.

But that wasn't the reason he decided to give in. He gave in because he could suffer anything for the sake of his children. He could even suffer through a brief consultation with a certain blue-eyed drill sarg—*image consultant.*

"So, what does this gift certificate get me?"

"Excuse me?"

"The gift certificate for the style analysis," Devon said patiently. "I want to use it. What do I get?"

Silence. And then, "The initial assessment. You fill out a questionnaire and then we discuss the results."

"How long does that take?"

"About two hours."

"That's it?"

Caitlin blinked. "For that...portion. Most people decide after that whether they want to take advantage of some of our other services."

Call him a glutton for punishment, but he was actually going to ask. "Like what?"

"Like achieving the right look as it pertains to a person's professional goals and lifestyle roles. Finding the appropriate clothing styles for um, specific body types." To Devon's fascination, the color in her cheeks deepened. "Choosing an appropriate hairstyle and appropriate clothing."

Devon got it. Appropriate. The secret weapon for success. "Okay."

"Okay, what?"

"Okay to everything you just said."

Something that looked like panic sparked in her eyes. "Maybe you should just make an appointment for the assessment. The rest is rather…expensive."

"How expensive?"

"I charge one hundred and twenty dollars an hour."

The air emptied out of Devon's lungs. His attorney hadn't charged near that amount. "No pro bono work?"

She didn't smile at the joke. "Mr. Walsh—"

"Call me Devon. We are going to be working together."

"Fine." Her husky voice crackled. "I'll set up an appointment and have Sabrina call you."

"Great. I hope you can be a little bit flexible with my schedule. Things get kind of hairy at home sometimes." Speaking of which… Devon realized he'd been gone a lot longer than he'd originally planned. "I have to run. I promised the kids I'd be home to make supper."

"Why are you doing this?" Caitlin's voice stopped him as he reached the door.

When Devon turned around, she hadn't moved. He had no idea how to answer the question, so he asked one of his own. "Jenny didn't really take second place in the contest, did she?"

The flicker of guilty surprise in Caitlin's eyes gave her away.

Bingo.

He smiled. "That's why."

Chapter Five

"That's why." Caitlin repeated Devon's cryptic words as she fumbled with the key to her apartment. For some odd reason, her hands hadn't stopped trembling since she'd closed up IMAGEine.

She blamed it on the drop in evening temperatures.

Mr. Darcy met her on the other side of the door, his ragged ears twitching a silent reprimand.

"Don't blame me." Caitlin shrugged off her coat and headed toward the kitchen. "Blame Devon Walsh. He's the reason your dinner is late."

The cat darted between her feet and cut in front of her, upsetting her balance and almost pitching her headfirst into the granite countertop on the breakfast bar. "We've talked about this before. If you kill me, there will be no one to feed you."

Caitlin shook the contents of a gourmet can of cat food into a ceramic dish near the refrigerator and rubbed her knuckles against the sensitive spot under Mr. Darcy's furry chin, a gesture which never failed to earn his forgiveness.

"At least one of us is happy," she muttered, putting off her own dinner to seek solace in her favorite chair overlooking the Mississippi River. Her apartment building had been an abandoned warehouse before a developer saw its potential and converted it into a series of trendy loft apartments.

She stared down at the dark ribbon of water and tried to figure out what had happened in the past hour.

Caitlin hadn't expected Devon to actually turn in the gift certificate for a free style analysis. The only reason she'd sent the silly thing in the first place was to make good on the first "prize" that came to mind after she'd made an executive decision to withdraw Jennifer's entry.

A decision Dawn Gallagher was still lamenting over. Caitlin knew their second choice would work out just as well but Dawn didn't think anyone else could compare to a "Mr. Makeover."

Guilt tugged briefly at Caitlin's conscience. The only explanation she'd given the *Twin City Trends'* style editor was that Devon was too busy to be involved in the makeover contest. Maybe he hadn't exactly *said* those words, but they had to be true. A single dad raising three kids...*while writing the next great American novel.*

What had she gotten herself into?

Devon didn't really want her help. He'd swallowed his pride because of his children. And it was easy to see that the man was going to be a rebel. The "I hope you can be flexible with my schedule" comment was the first gauntlet he'd thrown down.

Caitlin picked up a tasseled pillow and buried her head in it.

"He's not the only one with a schedule," she complained. "I have a schedule, too. And it's booked solid through the first of the year."

"Cait?"

Caitlin dropped the pillow and jackknifed into a sitting position at the sound of a muffled voice behind her. "Don't you ever knock?"

"Why should I?" Her sister Meghan grinned. "I have a key."

"Number four on my list of mistakes," Caitlin said under her breath.

"I didn't think you made mistakes—what were the first three? I promise I won't tell Evie." Meghan flopped down on the couch and Caitlin caught a glimpse of knee-high beaded moccasins under Meghan's long skirt.

She groaned. "Moccasins, Megs? You're killing me here."

"Aren't they great?" Meghan hiked up the hem on her tiered khaki skirt to show them off. "Cade bought them for me."

"I don't believe it. What have you done to the poor man?"

"The same thing I'm trying to do to you."

"Drive me crazy?"

"No, silly. Break you out of the first-born overachiever mold. Help you lighten up a little." Meghan swung her legs over the side of the ivory leather sofa and adjusted the pillows behind her back.

"Make yourself comfortable," Caitlin said dryly.

"Thanks." Meghan chuckled when Caitlin rolled her eyes. "Where's Mr. Darcy?"

"Sulking. Dinner was late."

"Poor baby. Did you get held up by work or traffic?"

Caitlin hesitated as Devon's face flashed in her mind. She'd only met him twice and yet somehow her memory was able to retrieve every one of his features with stunning clarity.

Meghan tilted her head, sending a mass of strawberry blonde curls tumbling over one shoulder. "Should I repeat the question?"

"Work." As much as she hated to admit it, Devon Walsh had officially become *work*. What was she going to do about him? Or more important, what was she going to do *with* him....

"Wow." Meghan's voice infiltrated her thoughts.

"What?"

"You were daydreaming."

Caitlin's fingers curled into the pillow. "Don't be silly."

Meghan leaned forward, studying her with something that

could only be termed as fascination. "And for a second there, you had The Look."

"What look?"

"*The* Look. You know, the one a woman gets in her eyes when she's thinking about a certain guy."

"Please." Caitlin vaulted out of the chair. "Have you eaten supper? Because I've got some leftover seafood fettuccine—"

"You. Are. Blushing." Meghan jumped up and blocked her escape route.

"Megs—"

"Who is he? Have you told Evie—" Meghan pushed Caitlin down on the sofa and plunked down beside her. Bringing them nose to nose.

"*No!*" At times like this, Caitlin questioned her decision to live in the same city as her younger sibling. "Was there a specific reason you stopped over or—"

Meghan clapped her hands together, effectively drowning Caitlin out. "Oooh, that means I get to tell her."

"There isn't anything to tell," Caitlin ground out. "He's a new client. A *client*. That's all. And the only reason I was—" she hated to admit it "—*thinking* about him was because he was the last appointment of the day."

The last *unscheduled* appointment of the day. And if Caitlin would have known how it was going to turn out, she would have made sure Sabrina sent him on his merry way. Sans gift certificate!

"A client." Meghan's shoulders drooped. "Really?"

"Really." Caitlin sounded so convincing, she almost believed it herself.

"Oh. Sorry, it's just that we—" Meghan bit down on her lower lip to prevent the rest of the words from spilling out.

Not that it mattered. Caitlin could guess what she'd been about to say.

They didn't want her to feel left out.

Both her sisters had found love within the past year and a half and their father, Patrick, teasingly took the credit for both successful matches. Even though Caitlin knew it had to be a total coincidence that Patrick's hobby—finding lost family heirlooms—had inadvertently led to both her sisters meeting the men they'd fallen in love with.

Another reason to limit the number of visits to Cooper's Landing! She didn't want her father pulling her into any of his crazy schemes. Or playing matchmaker for the only single daughter left in the McBride family.

"It's okay. Bask guilt-free in the glow of your own happiness," Caitlin said. "You know I don't have time for a relationship."

"You won't *make* time for a relationship," Meghan countered. "And Mr. Darcy, as much as I love him, doesn't count."

"Ah, Megs—why did you say you stopped over?"

"I didn't," Meghan said brightly. "But since you brought it up, fettuccine sounds good."

"Great." Caitlin hopped to her feet again and escaped to the kitchen, grateful for the distraction.

She loved her sister dearly but she didn't want to talk about Devon Walsh. She didn't want to *think* about Devon Walsh. There'd been no daydreaming. No *look*.

Meghan followed, Mr. Darcy draped over her arm like a trendy purse. "So, this guy…what's his name?"

Caitlin shot her a suspicious look. "Devon Walsh. Why do you ask?"

"Does he have a pocket protector? Thick glasses?"

"Meghan!" Caitlin choked back a laugh.

Humor backlit Meghan's eyes, making them appear more green than gray. "Black socks and sandals?"

"You're terrible."

"But am I right?"

Not even close, Caitlin thought, as her traitorous memory instantly downloaded a series of images of Devon Walsh.

"Not every guy who comes to IMAGEine is a nerd, you know."

"Uh-huh." Meghan didn't look convinced. "So that means he's a stuffy exec who wants a raise."

"Someone like Cade?" Caitlin asked wickedly.

"Cade isn't stuffy." Meghan paused. "Not once you get to know him anyway. Now, answer the question."

"Was there a question?" Caitlin stalled, banging pots and pans together in a pathetic attempt to distract her sister. Or better yet, maybe she had some cookies—Meghan's weakness—stashed somewhere.

"If your new client isn't a nerd or a suit, what's he like?"

Caitlin could tell she wasn't going to be able to avoid the conversation. Not without making Meghan suspicious as to *why* she was avoiding the conversation. "Long hair." Clean. And silky. "Five-o'clock shadow." The stubble did kind of work for him, though. "Dark eyes." Surrounded by laugh lines, although she hadn't seen much evidence of a sense of humor.

Caitlin had a flashback of his Ricky Ricardo impersonation and smiled to herself. When she glanced at Meghan, her sister had a thoughtful look on her face.

Warning!

"He hired me for a simple style analysis."

"So, there's potential."

"Absolutely not," Caitlin said firmly. "He's a *writer,* so he probably has the brooding, tortured artistic temperament…no offense, Megs…and I'm pretty sure we don't have a *thing* in common—"

"Um, Cait?" Meghan interrupted her gently. "I wasn't talking about *that* kind of potential. I meant potential in a *professional* sense."

Caitlin blinked. "Of course you were. Because anything else

would be ridiculous. A man who thinks suede elbow patches are still in style—" Caitlin realized she was rambling. *Rambling!* For the second time that day it felt as if the ground had suddenly shifted beneath her. The first time, of course, being when she'd walked into the reception area—in her stocking feet—and found Devon waiting for her....

Stay in control, Caitlin.

"I'm sure I have some Oreos. Somewhere." Caitlin launched a search-and-rescue mission in the pantry. Searching for cookies, rescuing herself from Meghan's knowing look.

"Take your time. I'm, ah, going to slip out and make a quick phone call."

Caitlin took one look at the mischievous sparkle in her sister's eyes and stifled a groan.

Of course she was.

"Watcha doing, Dad?" Brady and Josh's heads popped up over the back of the couch.

Devon didn't quite know how to answer the question.

Pacing? Dreading the next hour while looking forward to it at the same time? Because the contradiction that he was looking forward to seeing Caitlin again while knowing he shouldn't be looking forward to seeing her was making him...pace.

"Do you remember Ms. McBride? The lady who came over to talk to Jenny last week?"

Josh nodded. "She's the one who picked up Sunny."

The awe in his son's voice rankled. "She *did* scream."

"But she picked her up anyway."

"Very cool," Brady chimed in.

Devon decided not to debate the issue. When it was two against one, a person had to choose his battles wisely.

"*Anyway,* Ms. McBride is coming over this morning to help

me—" Devon paused, unsure how to describe why Caitlin was coming over.

"She's going to ask him some questions so he'll know what clothes look best on him." Jenny stepped out from behind the drapes.

Devon hadn't known she was there.

"Thank you." He winked at his daughter, who offered a hesitant smile before glancing away.

Devon tried to hide his disappointment at her response.

The boys, who'd been three years old when Ashleigh had taken them to Europe, had fewer memories of him than Jenny, yet they'd started to relax in his presence. To seek out his company.

But his daughter…she remained a mystery.

The counselor Devon had talked with had encouraged him to give Jenny the time and space she needed to grieve her mother's death. Devon got that. But even though his parental instincts were a bit rusty, he had the feeling other emotions lay buried beneath the veneer of sorrow in his daughter's eyes.

Devon had no idea what would unlock the secrets in Jenny's heart. And until recently, he'd started to doubt he was the right person for the job.

The night after Vickie had called, threatening to contest the custody arrangement, Devon had lain awake for hours. Not planning a legal strategy but wrestling with the reality that the kids, especially Jenny, *might* be better off with living with their aunt.

After all, his children knew their Aunt Vickie better than they knew their own father. Ashleigh and Vickie had always been close. So close that Ashleigh had hired her sister as her personal assistant when her modeling career began to take off. They'd traveled together. Spent holidays together. While Devon had to be content with long-distance phone calls and letters, Vickie had had the advantage of frequent visits with the children; knowing what went on in their day-to-day lives.

The boys, Devon had reasoned, might choose to stay with him, but Jenny would probably benefit from a woman's influence in her life. A woman would understand her emotions....would know what an adolescent girl needed.

He'd been praying for wisdom and guidance ever since Vickie's phone call. And just when Devon had almost convinced himself that his children would be better off with someone they knew and loved—not a man who was almost a stranger to them—there'd been a breakthrough.

We want to stay with you.

We. Plural.

While he couldn't deny the glimmer of hope that Jenny's simple statement had created that day, Devon also couldn't deny there was a truckload of irony in the situation. The makeover contest hadn't only revealed Jenny's feelings. It had brought Caitlin McBride into their lives.

As if on cue, the doorbell rang.

Chapter Six

Caitlin tried to focus on what Jenny was saying, but the closer they got to the parlor, the more wobbly her ankles felt. And wobbling in three-inch heels just wasn't...safe.

But neither were house calls.

But here you go, Caitlin thought. *Breaking your own rules.*

Working on the weekends wasn't the problem—for a lot of her clients, that was only time they were free—but it was a condition of IMAGEine's contract that unless she was shopping with a client, she met with them at her office. Unfortunately, Devon hadn't signed the contract. Yet. At the moment it was folded up inside her purse, waiting for his signature.

Caitlin didn't consider it necessary to visit a client's home because she discovered all she needed to know in the questionnaire.

The questionnaire was also folded up inside her purse.

But when Sabrina had talked to Devon on the phone to schedule his appointment, she'd claimed that he couldn't wait three weeks for his style analysis. And because he didn't want to leave the children, could Caitlin please come to his home instead of meeting at the office?

Caitlin had reluctantly agreed. Because she had a sinking suspicion as to why Devon didn't want to put off their meeting.

From the tiny bits of information Jenny shared in the essay she'd written and listening in on the conversation in the parlor that morning, Caitlin had pieced together an unsettling picture. An aunt named Vickie wanted custody of Devon's children. The children wanted to stay with their father. And judging from the fact that Devon was willing to hire her—an image consultant— at his daughter's urging, he wanted them to be together, too.

What Caitlin wasn't sure about was whether Devon should have them.

The dilapidated state of the house, outside as well as in, was a dead giveaway that Devon's assertion that he "made a living" as a writer was definitely a stretch of the imagination. And even though the guarded look in his eyes disappeared when he interacted with his children, Caitlin knew she hadn't been wrong when she'd pointed out the chip on his shoulder. In fact, she had the strangest feeling that Devon's edgy looks and choice of clothing were almost…deliberate.

A rebellion of some sort.

Against what? Caitlin wasn't sure, but whatever the reason, it didn't exactly fit the criteria for Father of the Year.

"…I like your bag."

Jenny's voice snapped Caitlin back to reality.

Not that she'd been daydreaming, of course.

"Thank you. I'll let you in on a little secret—I made it." Caitlin smiled down at the girl.

"Cool."

"It's easy… Do you know how to knit?"

Jenny shook her head, a pensive look in her eyes. Once again Caitlin was struck by their unusual color. Unusual and yet…oddly familiar, although she couldn't put her finger on the reason why.

The girl was going to be a beauty, no doubt about it. Like an artist's first sketch, the lines were already in place—a few more years and time and maturity would fill in the rest.

Based on experience, Caitlin knew the link between childhood and adolescence could be as precarious as a suspension bridge.

Would Devon know how to navigate his daughter through the difficult transition that would take place in the next few years? Would he understand the source of her insecurities? Provide a safe place for her to get to know herself?

Get a grip, Caitlin, she reminded herself firmly. Once this appointment with Devon was over, she'd move on to the next client.

That's what she did.

Caitlin followed Jenny into the parlor and her pulse skipped into an irregular beat at the sight of Devon standing beside the sofa. He wore loose-fitting jeans, a faded Minnesota Vikings sweatshirt and a frown that told her he was already regretting their business partnership.

That made two of them.

She resisted the urge to rub her damp palms down the front pockets of her patterned wool slacks. "Mr. Walsh."

"Ms. McBride." He matched her formal greeting, but there was a glint of humor in his eyes as he glanced down at her feet.

Caitlin felt her cheeks get warm at the subtle reminder of their last meeting. Drat the man. "Let's get started," she said briskly. "I'll need you to fill out this brief questionnaire first, and then we'll talk about the results."

Devon accepted the paperwork with a resigned sigh and spread it out on the coffee table. Jenny perched next to him, her chin cupped in the palm of her hand as she peered over his shoulder.

Caitlin left them alone and took a lap around the room; pausing to look out the window overlooking the spacious side yard that had, she guessed, been a garden once upon a time. A thick mat of colorful leaves covered the ground and ivy, tinted brown by the recent killing frost, wove between the gaps in the iron fence like a tapestry, forming a shield between the Walsh's yard and their neighbor's.

Caitlin's brow furrowed. If Devon didn't want to put the time and energy into maintaining the house and grounds, why not simply invest in a condo like she had, where the grounds crew took care of everything?

She resumed her self-guided tour, noticing large, old-fashioned iron heat grates on the floor and a trio of faded squares on the wall where pictures had once hung. The room could have benefited from a fresh coat of paint…

"I'm finished."

In five minutes? Not possible. Most of her clients took at least an hour to complete the questionnaire.

"You can't be—" Caitlin turned. And almost collided with Devon, who'd snuck up behind her.

She teetered and one of his hands closed around her elbow while the other molded around the curve of her waist to steady her.

The warmth of his fingers burned straight through her silk blouse and Caitlin jerked away, almost losing her balance again in the process.

"Okay?" For the second time, Devon stared down at her feet. But when he started to kneel down, as concerned as a coach with an injured player, Caitlin backpedaled out of his reach.

"You're finished already?" Why did her breathing sound as if she'd just run half the length of a football field?

"It wasn't quite as complex as the ACT I took in high school. A close second, though."

Caitlin refused to smile. She caught Jenny's eye across the room and the girl gave a subtle shake of her head. A few seconds later, as Caitlin skimmed the questionnaire, she discovered why.

"You didn't fill out the bottom portion."

"That's because it doesn't pertain to me."

"Doesn't—" Caitlin silently counted to five. "Every question pertains to everyone." Since she'd designed the assessment herself, she knew it was the truth.

Devon's jaw turned to granite under the stubble. "I'm not interested in discussing my professional goals."

With you.

The unspoken words hung in the air between them.

For someone who'd hired her, Devon was being unreasonably stubborn, Caitlin thought. Maybe he didn't understand the intent behind the questions.

"Your professional goals figure into the overall image you want to project," she said carefully. "You mentioned you're a writer. If you have an opportunity to meet with an agent or a publisher, you're going to have to convince them to take yourself and your work seriously. Your clothes—and your attitude—have to communicate that you believe in yourself. Trust me when I say that the starving-artist look only works for the ones who aren't."

Starving artist.

Devon suppressed a smile. Over Caitlin's head, he saw Jenny's eyes widen in surprise and he put his finger to his lips.

"I'll keep that in mind."

"Good." Caitlin's smooth forehead wrinkled as she scanned the rest of his answers. "You didn't describe a typical day."

"No, I didn't." Maybe because none of his days could be described as typical?

"Well, I just need to jot a few things down. You said you work at home. And you enjoy…remodeling." Caitlin's sharp, blue-eyed gaze swept the interior of the room doubtfully.

Point taken, Devon thought wryly. "That's right."

His remodeling efforts had pretty much ground to a halt after the kids moved in, but he tried to find time in the evenings to tackle smaller projects. Not that he needed to bore Caitlin with those insignificant details, however. Not when it was clear she'd already decided he was a loser.

It explained why she'd risked breaking both ankles leaping away from him when he'd touched her. She wasn't wearing a ring on her left hand, but Devon had a hunch he knew exactly what type of guy would measure up to Caitlin's exacting standards. Someone as well groomed and well behaved as a standard poodle at the Westminster dog show.

Out of the corner of his eye, Devon saw Josh and Brady, who'd disappeared the moment they'd heard Caitlin's voice in the hallway, slip back into the room and duck behind the oak buffet. Their stealthy movements and the dark sunglasses they wore told Devon they'd morphed into Marty and Matt Ransom, junior detectives.

"Mmm." Caitlin turned to the next page and the paper rattled as she raised accusing eyes to his. "You didn't describe your social life, either. Our goal is to come up with an overall look that works *with* your lifestyle. Every part of it. How am I supposed to help you accomplish that when you—"

"He doesn't have a social life," Jenny interrupted, her tone apologetic. "He has us."

Surprised and pleased that his daughter had spoken up in his defense, Devon gave Jenny a cheerful wink. "More than a fair trade-off, in my opinion."

Caitlin stared at him. "But you must do…something. An occasional movie? Dinner out with friends?"

Friends?

The question pressed against a wound on Devon's heart that hadn't quite healed. That particular word had been missing from his vocabulary since he'd moved to Minneapolis. Several of the people he'd thought of as friends had openly discussed his situation with reporters to claim their fifteen minutes of fame.

Devon had operated on survival mode after the divorce and during the two-year legal battle that followed. The one that finally ended with a judge's decision to allow Ashleigh to keep the children with her in Europe.

After the attention that media circus created, guarding his privacy had become more than a necessity, it had become a habit.

"He makes us spaghetti." Josh emerged from his hiding place and sidled over to his father's side, Brady trailing along behind him. "And the noodles don't stick together anymore."

"The sauce doesn't taste burned, either."

"Wow. Thanks for the vote of confidence, guys." Devon clamped a hand down on each sandy brown head and ruffled their hair. "But I don't think Ms. McBride is here to judge my cooking skills." He slanted a look at her. "Are you?"

A smile shimmered in Caitlin's eyes, and the air emptied out of Devon's lungs. Was it his imagination, or had her expression softened while his children praised his spaghetti-making skills?

"You'll have to finish the questionnaire to find out the answer to that," she said coolly.

Okay, definitely his imagination.

"I did finish it."

"Fine." Caitlin sighed. "Let's skip the professional goals and jot down a few things in the 'typical day' category."

"You're conceding?" Devon pretended to be shocked.

The elusive smile came and went in Caitlin's eyes again, making Devon wonder what it would take to coax it out of hiding completely.

Probably a guy in Armani with reservations at an exclusive restaurant, a taunting voice in his head replied.

"It's called a compromise, Mr. Walsh." Caitlin leaned forward and the exotic fragrance she favored stirred the air. "Because it's important to set a good example for the children, don't you agree?"

He agreed. But Devon couldn't resist imitating Caitlin's sigh as he took the questionnaire from her and dropped into a vacant chair. Josh and Brady flanked his sides like bookends.

"I'll help you, Dad," Brady whispered. "I keep track of everything."

"I know you do, kiddo." Devon forced a smile. He had a hunch that his son's high-vigilance in time management was the result of punishments he'd received for being habitually late for class.

And even though he hadn't come across *that* particular scenario in a parenting book, Devon went with his gut and didn't make a big deal out of it. Instead, he prayed that Brady would eventually feel secure enough to put the stopwatch aside.

"We should write the stuff down from yesterday because today isn't done yet," Brady pointed out.

But writing down today's "stuff" would be so much faster, Devon wanted to argue. He nodded instead, careful to keep his expression as solemn as his son's. "Yesterday, it is."

"You got up at five-thirty to take a shower—"

Devon gulped. Morning grooming definitely fell under the Too Much Information Act!

"Let's just start with breakfast, okay, bud?"

"Okay." Brady shrugged agreeably. "You made pancakes at six thirty-five."

"And then we cleaned up the syrup on the floor," Josh added.

Devon suppressed a smile. Of course Josh, being the one responsible for the syrup fiasco, had remembered that little glitch in his morning.

"You took Rosie for a walk around the block at seven-fifteen—"

"No, he had to clean up her mess first."

Devon closed his eyes at the reminder. He didn't dare look at Caitlin but her choke of laughter—no, it had to have been horror—told him that she'd tuned in to their conversation.

A brilliant idea struck him. "Jenny—why don't you get Ms. McBride something to drink? In the *kitchen?* I think there might be some cookies left, too."

"Okay." Jenny smiled shyly at Caitlin. "Do you like chocolate chip?"

"They happen to be my favorite. Did you make them?"

"I helped Dad—" Caitlin fell in step with Jenny as they made their way across the room and Devon exhaled in relief.

"You wrote for three hours and twenty-seven minutes," Brady went on. "With a five-minute break for a snack."

Devon glanced at his son in disbelief. He didn't think anyone had noticed his brief foray into the kitchen.

Josh refused to be left out of the loop. "And then you made grilled-cheese sandwiches."

"Twice. He burned the first ones, remember?"

"I'm not writing that down," Devon muttered.

This time, Devon could have sworn he heard Caitlin chuckle before she disappeared.

Chapter Seven

Caitlin followed Jenny into the kitchen and tried to hide her surprise.

The gleaming stainless-steel appliances looked new but the stone fireplace and butler's pantry remained, charming reminders that the house had its origins in an earlier era. Five mismatched chairs circled a pedestal table piled high with books. The hickory cabinets, stripped down to the original wood, would be beautiful when they were refinished.

The whole room, though a little different in style, reminded Caitlin of the kitchen in the house she'd grown up in. The McBrides' rambling, two-story home in an older suburban neighborhood would never have been featured in a decorating magazine, but it had radiated a warm and welcoming atmosphere nonetheless.

Laura McBride, a police officer, worked the day shift so she could be home when school let out for the day. After their homework was finished, Caitlin's mother assigned each of the girls a specific task to help with supper, smiling patiently as the three of them vied for her attention.

Caitlin's lips curved at the bittersweet memory.

Laura had always encouraged her daughters and supported their dreams. Meghan's artwork had decorated the refrigerator while the kitchen table often performed double duty as a lab for Evie's science experiments. And even though Caitlin's own interests and abilities had been drastically different from her mother's, an adventurous outdoor enthusiast, Laura had signed up to take sewing classes with Caitlin when her oldest daughter showed an interest in designing and making her own clothing.

Caitlin had already been living on her own when Laura died unexpectedly in the line of duty, but she still felt the void of her mother's absence as if it had happened yesterday.

Caitlin watched Jenny carefully select unbroken cookies from a plastic container and wondered again about the girl's mother. In the essay she'd sent in, all Jenny had said was that her mother was "gone." Caitlin's own experience with grief, however, allowed her to recognize it in others. The truth was evident in Jenny's eyes and the pain was still fresh.

Caitlin felt an unexpected tug on her heart. Not only for Jenny but for…Devon. Not only had the children lost their mother, he'd lost his wife.

"Would you like some hot chocolate, too?" Jenny held out a ragged piece of paper towel with two cookies cradled in the center.

Caitlin spotted an industrial-strength coffee pot on the counter. "You go ahead. I'll have coffee, if you don't think your dad will mind."

"He won't care." Jenny shrugged. "He drinks it all day."

At least they had one thing in common.

Caitlin swiftly dispatched that disturbing thought. Devon was a client. They didn't *need* to have anything in common!

She sat down at the table across from Jenny and moved a stack of books to the side. One of the titles caught her eye.

The Ransom Brothers and the Secret of the Fire Stone

The cover, depicting a shadowy silhouette standing outside

the window, reminded her of a modern day version of the Nancy Drew mysteries she'd read at Jenny's age.

"Do you like to read?" Caitlin asked.

Jenny's eyes lit up and she nodded. "Dad reads that one to us after supper. I like it but I'm reading the Narnia books by myself, too."

"I always enjoyed those." Caitlin picked up the mystery and saw the cover of a textbook underneath it. "My sister, Evie, is a science teacher."

"You have a sister?" Jenny sounded a little wistful.

"Two of them. Meghan is a photographer and Evie teaches middle school."

"I'm in seventh grade," Jenny said. "Science is okay, I guess, but I like history better. We're studying landforms right now, and Dad promised to help me make a working volcano."

"Are you going to enter it in a science fair?"

"Maybe. If they have one at our new school."

"New school?"

"Dad teaches us at home right now but we might go to New Hope Academy after Christmas. It's right next door to our church."

Caitlin tried not to let her astonishment show. She didn't have anything against parents teaching their children at home, she'd just never known a father who'd taken on that level of responsibility before. "Your dad teaches all *three* of you?"

"Sure. He's good at it," Jenny said blithely. "Especially English, 'cause he's a writer."

"Of course." Caitlin kept her voice neutral but she couldn't stifle her curiosity. "Has he always taught you…at home?"

"No." Jenny averted her gaze, but not before Caitlin caught a flash of sorrow in those copper eyes, as if the innocent question had peeled away a corner to reveal a lingering pain below the surface. "I went to a private school…before."

"Really? Which one?"

"St. Agnes."

"St. Agnes," Caitlin repeated, unable to place the name among the list of private schools she was familiar with in the Twin Cities area.

"It's in England," Jenny added, almost as an afterthought. *England?*

"Did your brothers go there—"

"Sorry to interrupt." Devon stood in the doorway. And he didn't look a bit sorry. He smiled at Jenny but Caitlin could have skated across the ice in his eyes when he glanced her way. "The questionnaire is officially complete. We don't want to take up any more of Ms. McBride's afternoon than necessary."

"Okay, Dad." Jenny glanced back and forth between the two adults in confusion, as if sensing the sudden tension crowding the air.

Devon exhaled quietly, forcing his fingers to loosen and uncurl before Jenny noticed they'd been fisted at his sides.

Was he kidding himself?

Was it possible to let Caitlin into their home—into their lives—without jeopardizing what he'd been working so hard to accomplish? Taking time to shelter his children while strengthening the tenuous threads that bound the family together?

Jenny's innocent comments had to have raised a hundred questions in Caitlin's mind.

Devon understood. Because when it came to his children, he still had a few dozen unanswered questions of his own.

He'd picked up on the subtle change in Jenny's voice when she'd mentioned St. Agnes.

When Devon had expressed concern about enrolling Jenny in a boarding school at such a young age, Ashleigh had accused him of being selfish and denying their children the opportunities they needed to succeed in life. If he wanted to enjoy any kind of relationship with Jenny and the boys in the future, he had to prove he wanted the best for them.

Devon had backed off. Partly because he'd assumed Ashleigh wouldn't force Jenny into something she didn't want to do and partly out of guilt. After all, wasn't his failed marriage proof that he hadn't had enough to offer?

Over the next few years, Devon had received infrequent but enthusiastic updates from Ashleigh about the children's friends and their wide range of activities and interests. Because his weekly telephone conversations with Jenny and the boys didn't contradict what Ashleigh told him, he'd believed the children were thriving in private school.

But what he'd found out not long after they'd moved in with him—and that only because he'd accidentally over-heard a conversation between Jenny and her brothers—was that Ashleigh's visits to see Jenny at St. Agnes had been brief and sporadic.

With a little casual digging, Devon learned the boys had been in a similar situation. Ashleigh, who'd traveled extensively and embraced her jet-set lifestyle, had hired a full-time nanny for preschoolers Josh and Brady. When the twins reached school age, she'd sent them to a boarding school, too. One that would, in her words, "adequately prepare them for college."

It had been difficult to get the boys to talk about their experience at school, but when Devon had pushed the issue at bedtime one night, Josh had finally spoken up. And he hadn't said a word about clubs or activities or friends. Instead, his simple description, straight out of the prep-school handbook, had chilled Devon's blood.

"It provides a rigorous academic program that fosters excellence in a disciplined environment. Don't you remember, Dad? Mom said you wanted us to go there."

And if that hadn't been enough to splinter Devon's heart into a zillion pieces, the sight of Brady, standing motionless near the window with tears in his eyes, had just about destroyed Devon.

Rigorous. Disciplined. He'd read between the lines and knew why the boys flinched whenever he caught them playing and why they acted more like miniature soldiers than curious, active nine-year-old boys.

It had taken Devon a while to move beyond the guilt that mushroomed out of Josh's stunning disclosure. And to turn over to God the anger he felt toward Ashleigh, who'd led the boys to believe their father had chosen that type of school.

Ashleigh had also failed to mention the children stayed at their respective schools over the holidays and that they attended a mind-boggling series of enrichment classes that consumed their entire summer vacation.

Summers they could have spent with him.

What tore him apart even more was the realization that not only didn't the children know him, they barely knew each other.

It was one of the reasons Devon had decided to homeschool. They would all benefit from some serious bonding time. The other reason, and one he hadn't shared with the children, had to do with the real need to keep them off the radar a little longer.

After Ashleigh died, the reporters' interest switched to the children she'd left behind. But by the time they located the private schools and began to badger the faculty for information, Devon already had the children safely back in the United States.

Now all he had to do was pray that he'd made the right decision by hiring Caitlin.

But who was he trusting? The woman whose loyalty seemed to be planted firmly in the roots of the business she'd started or the woman whose expression softened in response to his children's laughter?

During the uncomfortable silence that followed, Caitlin had the impression that Devon's stern Heathcliff impersonation had less to do with the questionnaire he'd been forced to fill out and more to do with Jenny talking about the school she'd attended.

Did he think she'd deliberately coaxed information from Jenny? The idea didn't sit well with her.

"I have to get back to the office." Caitlin rose to her feet and walked to the sink with her cup. "It will take me a day or two to evaluate the questionnaire and get back to you."

Devon's expression changed to surprise. "You have to go back to the office?"

"I work most weekends." Didn't everyone?

She turned on the faucet to rinse out the last few drops of coffee...and found herself on the receiving end of a shower.

Caitlin wasn't sure where the water was coming from, but in five seconds flat she felt as if she'd been pushed through a car wash. Without benefit of a car. Devon launched himself across the distance between them and turned the water off.

He quickly surveyed the damage and must have determined she was the worst casualty. "Jenny, get Ms. McBride a towel, please."

"I guess you should add the sink to your list of remodeling projects," Caitlin gasped, blotting the towel Jenny offered against her damp cheeks.

"The sink isn't broken," Devon muttered. "I'm pretty sure you fell into a booby trap meant for the evil Dr. Chamberlain."

Caitlin blinked. "The evil Dr. who?"

"Never mind." Devon grabbed a roll of paper towels, called for the boys and knelt to mop up the floor.

"Did you want something, Dad?" Josh and Brady appeared in the doorway and saw Caitlin—the soggy testimonial of an undercover operation gone awry.

She expected them to turn and bolt, but they charged into the kitchen.

"We're sorry, Ms. McBride. Are you okay? We didn't know *you'd* turn on the water." Their voices tumbled over each other.

Caitlin saw the remorseful expressions on the boys' faces and took pity on them. "It's okay." She dabbed at the water spots on her blouse. "It's only water. I won't melt."

"But your shirt looks funny now," Brady said.

"That's because it's silk." Devon closed his eyes briefly. "I'll pay the bill to have it cleaned."

"No, you won't." Caitlin caught a glimpse of her reflection in the toaster and suppressed a shudder. "The bill would cost more than the blouse. I bought it at Samantha's Attic."

Devon gave her a blank look.

"It's a consignment shop." And one of her favorite stores. "I think I paid five dollars for this one." She smiled down at Josh and Brady. "The only things I need are my coat and the questionnaire."

And a dignified exit, which was going to be a little more difficult to manage. She'd met her quota for embarrassing situations in the same month, and Devon Walsh had been there to witness them both!

"You have black stuff on your cheeks," Josh said.

Of course she did. "That would be my mascara."

"It makes you look like a rac—"

"Josh!" Devon cleared his throat.

Caitlin chuckled. "The package claimed it was waterproof, but I guess I never put it to the test before."

Devon didn't say anything and when she glanced at him, the searching look in his eyes sucked the air out of her lungs. It made her feel...vulnerable. Exposed. As if he wanted to discover what was going on *inside* her...

Caitlin turned away.

She never would have achieved the level of success she had if she wore her heart on her sleeve. People respected confidence. And strength. And no matter what Caitlin was feeling on the inside, that's what she made sure they saw on the *outside*.

She retreated to the parlor and Devon fell into step beside

her. As she gathered up her things, she was acutely aware of Devon's gaze on her.

"Cait?"

She wrinkled her nose. Only her family called her Cait!

"I'm sorry about the shower. Those kinds of things are part of my typical day, but you shouldn't have been caught in the crossfire between the Ransom brothers and Dr. Chamberlain."

Caitlin slid the questionnaire into a folder. "I grew up in an older home similar to this."

His expression became guarded. "And?"

"The heating grates on the floor…they transfer sounds very efficiently to other rooms in the house."

Devon's eyebrows rose in sudden understanding. "Sounds like…voices?"

"I thought it might be helpful to know…considering that Dr. Chamberlain *is* hopelessly outnumbered."

While Devon padded over to the heating grates and studied them, his expression a mixture of dawning understanding and disbelief, Caitlin took the opportunity to slip out of the room.

Chapter Eight

"She's been avoiding us, hasn't she, Evie?"

"It certainly appears that way."

Caitlin knew she shouldn't have answered the phone. But she had and now she had to live with the consequences of her folly. When she heard not one, but *both* of her sisters' chipper voices on the line, she'd been tempted to drop her headset out the car window.

If only it wouldn't be considered littering....

She checked her rearview mirror and changed lanes. "I am here, you know. Just in case you want to talk *to* me instead of about me."

"We'd love to talk to you," Meghan said reasonably. "But we haven't been able to get in touch with you."

"You're in touch with me now."

"She must be busy," Evie said.

"That's true." Meghan waited a beat. "Probably with a new client."

"Excuse me. Am I necessary to this conversation?" Caitlin demanded.

"Do you have a new client, Cait?" Evie was all sweetness and light.

Caitlin's teeth snapped together. "I always have new clients."

And she just happened to be on her way to see one right now. A tiny detail that her annoying siblings didn't need to know.

"Dad is getting worried because you aren't returning his calls, either," Meghan said.

Caitlin made a left turn onto the quiet street and her stomach did a flip when she saw the rippled roofline of a certain house at the end of the block. "What do you mean? I talked to him Saturday night."

"I know, But he mentioned you sounded...distracted," Evie said.

"Dis—" Caitlin's foot eased off the gas pedal as the over-whelming urge to turn the car around crashed over her. "—tracted?"

"Uh-huh," Meghan said dryly. "Kind of like the way you sound right now."

"Don't be silly. I'm not—" Caitlin spotted Jenny and her brothers on the other side of the fence, raking leaves into a gigantic pile, probably with the intent to jump in them. She and her sisters had enjoyed doing the same thing at that age.

"Caitlin?" Evie shouted in her ear. "Is everything all right? Where are you, anyway?"

"I'm fine." Caitlin addressed the first question and ignored the second. Not that she was being entirely honest about her state of mind. Several times on the way across town she'd been tempted to call Devon and cancel their appointment.

Her sisters had thwarted her chance. And even her car seemed to have a mind of its own. When she lifted her foot completely off the gas pedal, the vehicle glided alongside the curb. And sat there idling right in front of Devon Walsh's intimidating iron gate. "It's just...I should go. I have an appointment."

The children spotted her and waved, their faces breaking out into wide smiles. Some unidentifiable emotion stirred inside Caitlin. Mr. Darcy was the only one who looked that excited to see her and she had a sneaking suspicion it was only because her arrival was synonymous with dinner.

"But it's after five," Evie said.

Caitlin could almost picture the frown wrinkling her sister's forehead. The youngest McBride, who had a tendency to fuss over the rest of the family, definitely qualified as the mother hen of their sisterly brood. "I realize that, but I—"

The pile of leaves moved and Devon popped up out of the center. Leaves clung to his clothing and stuck to his hair and the unexpected sight wrenched a breathless laugh from her.

"Did she just laugh?" Meghan demanded.

"It sounded like it. Either that or she's choking. Caitlin, are you choking?"

"I'm not choking." Caitlin's lips curved into a smile when Josh and Brady sprinted to the gate to unlock it. For her. "But I have to go. My...client is waiting."

"Your new client? The one with potential?" Meghan asked irrepressibly.

"Goodbye, meddling sisters. And when you talk to Dad tonight, tell him that I *wasn't* distracted."

"She sounds a little distracted now," Meghan whispered. "Don't you think so, Evie?"

"At least she's not chok—"

Caitlin smiled as she shut the phone off.

Devon swiped at the leaves clinging to his sweater as he watched Caitlin's slim frame unfold from the driver's side of a posh little Mini Cooper.

She'd actually shown up.

Until the moment Devon had seen her car turn down the street, he'd had his doubts.

Josh and Brady competed to unlock the gate and as Caitlin stepped through, she paused a moment to say something to them. Whatever it was, both boys grinned and their chests puffed up like roosters.

Caitlin cinched the belt of her cream-colored wool coat more tightly around her waist as she approached. "Hello, Jennifer."

"Hi, Ms. McBride." Jenny hung back, but Devon didn't miss the sparkle in his daughter's eyes. He'd caught her looking down the street several times while they'd been playing in the leaves, and once again he wondered what it was about Caitlin McBride that drew Jenny out of her shell.

Even the boys had asked about her several times over the course of the afternoon. It had gotten to the point that Devon took them outside to rake leaves just to keep their hands busy and their minds occupied with something other than Caitlin's arrival.

It had worked for him. For a little while, anyway.

"Hi, Cait." Devon remembered the way her nose had wrinkled the last time he'd called her that, and he couldn't resist doing it again, just to see if it garnered the same results.

It did.

"Devon." Caitlin's gaze flickered over him. "You must be doing leaf identification. Very creative, by the way, doubling as your own flannel board."

Laughter spurted out before he could prevent it, but Josh came to his rescue.

"We're done with school for the day. We were just busy waiting for you."

"Dad made us play in the leaves." Brady consulted his watch. "For fifty-seven minutes."

"He made you, mmm?" Amazingly enough, Caitlin's lips

softened into a smile. "I'm sorry I kept you waiting. My sisters called right when I was leaving."

Josh nodded, his expression solemn. "That's okay. Dad says family comes first."

"Your dad is absolutely right." Caitlin shivered as another gust of wind picked up the leaves and sent them swirling into the air.

"Come in the house before you get frostbite. If you wore a shirt like this, you wouldn't be cold, you know." Devon was rocked by a sudden, irresistible urge to wrap his arm around her. Just to protect her from the wind.

He shoved his hands into his pockets instead.

"If I were wearing a shirt like that, I wouldn't be out in public," Caitlin said sweetly.

"I'm detecting an underlying prejudice against flannel," Devon muttered, holding the door open to let everyone troop past.

"Okay, you guys." He clapped his hands together. "Miss McBride and I have to complete Phase Two—"

"Can I help?" Jenny asked eagerly.

Devon hesitated. He didn't want his kids to put him on a pedestal and yet they didn't need to witness his utter humiliation, either. "For five minutes. And then you have to check the chore list before supper. Deal?"

Jenny beamed up at him. "Deal."

"Does this have something to do with clothes?" Brady wrinkled his nose.

"'Fraid so, bud."

"We'll be upstairs." The boys disappeared and Devon led the way to the parlor.

"Here are the six articles of clothing I wear the most. Just like you requested." Devon's smug expression dared her to find something wrong with them.

Caitlin ran a practiced eye over the clothing carefully arranged on the sofa. She might not understand the fluttery feeling in her stomach when she'd seen Devon pop out of the leaves, but *this* was familiar territory.

And it was worse than she expected.

"Where do you board your horse?"

Devon frowned. "I don't have a horse."

Caitlin tossed a hunter-green-and-blue plaid shirt with pearl buttons to the side. "Then you don't need this."

Jenny giggled, then clapped her hand over her mouth.

"Hey—"

"Or this." Caitlin added the shirt's red-and-black checkered twin to the beginning of a pile she guessed would grow very quickly.

"There's still a lot of wear in those," Devon protested.

"Great. Someone else can wear them." Caitlin examined a ragged pair of blue jeans with a missing back pocket. She folded them up and set them to the side.

"We're keeping those?" Devon's expression was hopeful.

"No. The shirts are going to the local thrift store. And this—" she waved a hand over the jeans "—is the rag pile."

"Rag pile? No way. I just broke those in."

"That explains the Western shirts."

"Do you insult all your clients like this?"

Caitlin had to think about that. "No," she finally said, surprised by the answer. "Just you."

"I'm flattered."

"I do understand your need for comfort—"

"Really?" Devon directed a skeptical look at her favorite pair of heels. Which Caitlin ignored.

"You're at home during the day and you spend a lot of time on your computer. You don't venture out much." Rarely at all, based on what the children had said. "But it's possible to update your…casual…look and not sacrifice comfort."

"People pay a lot of money for jeans with slight imperfections," Devon pointed out.

"Slight imperfections, yes. Missing back pockets, no."

"She's right, Dad," Jenny ventured.

Devon exhaled noisily and crossed his arms. Caitlin chalked it up as a small victory. When he wasn't looking, she gave Jenny the thumbs-up sign. She grinned back.

"I saw that." Devon rolled his eyes. "It's a conspiracy. A plot to change me."

"A common misconception that I battle on a daily basis. Image consultants don't try to change you—we help reflect the real you." Caitlin scanned the rest of the clothing. "Where's the sweater you were wearing the day I met you? The one with the suede elbow patches?"

The one that should have been recycled into potholders.

"That's Dad's writing sweater," Jenny said.

"Writing sweater?"

"Jenny—" Color reddened Devon's cheeks.

"He has to wear it or he can't think."

Caitlin tilted her head. "Interesting."

"I suppose that'll end up in your file," Devon muttered.

Caitlin was a little unsettled by the fact that he knew she had a file. She gave up on the sweater—for now.

"You can keep this." She held up the lone item from his closet that had passed inspection.

"You're kidding me."

"Not at all."

"You discard perfectly good *collared* shirts and then tell me I can wear a T-shirt that I bought for five dollars at a Renaissance fair. Ten years ago."

"The color and the playbill silk-screened on the front isn't dated, it's retro. Not everyone could pull it off, but you shouldn't have a problem given that you're a writer. What *do* you write, by the way?"

"Different things," Devon said vaguely. "Did you want a cup of coffee? Something to eat?"

"No, thank you. What kind of different things? Fiction? Nonfiction?"

"Maybe I write poetry."

"Poetry."

"You don't like poetry?" That captivating twitch worked the corner of Devon's lips again and short-circuited Caitlin's train of thought.

"I don't have a lot of spare time to read." And if she did, it would be the dog-eared copy of *Pride and Prejudice* she kept on the nightstand.

"So now we go shopping for appropriate clothes, right?"

"Shop—" Caitlin choked on the word. "I can give you some advice on what to purchase, of course."

"I thought personal shopping was one of the services that IMAGEine offers."

"It is." Caitlin glanced at Jenny. She didn't want to embarrass him in front of his daughter by questioning the numbers in his bank account. The gift certificate covered the initial style analysis and she'd already decided not to charge him for the additional time she was spending with him that evening. "But shopping is an additional cost, remember?"

"And I mentioned that I'm going to need more help than the style analysis, remember?"

"You want me to go shopping with you?" More time with Devon. Caitlin's pulse skipped a beat.

"No, I don't like the crowds this time of year. Could we order some things online? Tomorrow evening?"

"I really can't do that." Caitlin tried to come up with a reason why. Other than the obvious. That close proximity to Devon did strange things to her heart. Distracted her. And she couldn't afford to be distracted—not when she gave a hundred percent to building her reputation. "The only reason I came over tonight was because you said you needed the wardrobe analysis as soon as possible."

"Cait?" Devon's voice was as soft as cashmere. "All that's left of my wardrobe is a T-shirt. I'm pretty sure that means I need some help...*as soon as possible.*"

Chapter Nine

"Caitlin's here."

Two simple words that had a profound impact on Devon's peace of mind.

"I'll be down in a minute." Because he was putting off the inevitable.

You were the one who insisted on an online shopping spree, buddy. Now it's time to face the Armani.

The boys thundered past Devon as he made his way down the stairs to find Jenny already opening the front door to greet their guest.

Once again, Caitlin must have come directly from the office. Devon felt a twinge of guilt for insisting she make another house call. But hadn't she matter-of-factly told him that she worked weekends, too?

Devon briefly wondered if she took any time for herself. And if she did, what her interests were.

Not the same as yours, Dev, a mocking voice butted in. She's probably a see-and-be-seen person, not a homebody like you.

Still, Devon couldn't help but smile at the bemused expression on Caitlin's face as his children gave her a recap of their day. At the same time.

He waded into the mayhem. "Can I take your coat?"

Caitlin hesitated and then gave a small nod of acquiescence. "Thank you."

Devon slipped the leather coat off her shoulders and when he saw what was underneath it, his heart dropped into his shoes like a stone.

Judging from what Caitlin was wearing—an elegant, figure-hugging black cocktail dress dusted with sparkly stuff—the Walsh household was merely a brief stopover on her way to an evening out on the town.

"That's a pretty dress," Jenny said. "Are you going to a party?"

Caitlin smiled. "No, just dinner with friends."

"Okay, guys." Devon clapped his hands to cut off any further questions. He really didn't want to get into a question-and-answer session about Caitlin's dinner with friends. "Caitlin and I have some work to do and so do you."

"Dad read in some book that responsibility builds charac-ter," Josh lamented.

"We're going to have *a lot* of character," Brady added.

They slunk away, and for the first time, Devon saw the look of shock on Caitlin's face.

"What?"

"Your…shirt." Her voice sounded huskier than normal and her gaze flitted around the foyer like a butterfly unsure of where to light.

Devon glanced down. "Do you like it? The fashion police told me it was retro."

"But what happened to the…*sleeves?*"

"They were a little tight, so I cut them off. I did mention that I bought this shirt ten years ago, right? I was thinner in my early twenties."

Caitlin frowned and Devon had a sudden inkling why Jenny had squeaked when she'd caught him in the kitchen earlier that morning, attacking the fabric with a pair of dull scissors.

He sighed. "It's not retro anymore, is it?"

"No."

"Thrift store?"

She raised an eyebrow.

"Rag pile?"

"Rag pile."

Devon winced. "Do you see why I need you?"

"Oh, that was obvious the moment I met you," Caitlin said tartly and started down the hall, the filmy layered skirt swinging gently with each step. The light caught on the flecks of glitter in her dress, reminding Devon of snow sparkling in the moonlight.

Devon's eyes rolled toward the ceiling.

Any more of that mush and you *will* be able to call yourself a poet, he chided himself.

Caitlin walked away, counting each step in an attempt to dispel the image lodged in her head: the sight of Devon's mutilated shirt and the muscular arms that mutilated shirt showed off to perfection.

She found herself wishing he'd put the flannel one back on.

A telephone jarred the sudden silence and Devon caught up with her. "Do you mind if I answer that?" he asked. "I've been…expecting a call."

"Not at all." Caitlin caught a glimpse of Jenny lingering halfway up the staircase and let Devon stride past her.

Caitlin changed direction, sensing that Devon's daughter wanted to talk to her. Not that she claimed to understand young people, but something in the girl's pensive expression tugged at Caitlin's emotions.

"What's on your list?"

Jenny's nose wrinkled. "It's my turn to clean the fishbowl."

Caitlin picked her way slowly up the stairs, keeping a wary eye on the lumps in the worn carpet runner. "I had an aquarium when I was your age, too. My sisters and I named the fish after characters in the books we were reading at the time."

Jenny laughed, caught herself and spread her fingers over her mouth to cover her braces.

Caitlin's heart went out to the girl. "Why don't you introduce me to your fish while we wait for your dad?"

"Sure." Jenny's face brightened.

Caitlin followed her the rest of the way up the stairs and the moment her foot touched the landing, she realized something was…different.

Where the lumpy runner ended, a plush carpet in a soft shade of autumn-brown began.

Unease trickled down Caitlin's spine as she studied the artwork arranged on the pristine eggshell walls. Devon had displayed a private collection of drawings and paintings—all rendered by his children and all of them professionally framed.

It was possible, she thought, that she hadn't been completely fair when she'd expressed doubt about Devon's remodeling skills.…

And then she saw Jenny's room.

It was absolutely…beautiful.

Pale peach walls cast a warm glow around the spacious room while the hardwood floor, softened by soft-looped throw rugs, gleamed in the lamplight.

The large dormer overlooking the street had been transformed into a cozy reading nook, piled high with an array of pillows that matched the saltwater-taffy pastels on the canopy bed.

The rocking chair and the blanket chest, both crowded with a friendly contingent of stuffed animals, appeared to be hand-crafted. An oval mirror, draped with colorful scarves and bandannas, stood in the corner next to the bed.

Someone had even taken the time to stencil a cute Parisian café scene on one of the walls.

Devon?

Caitlin swallowed. Hard.

"Do you like it?" Jenny asked anxiously.

"I do." Caitlin forced a smile. "It's perfect, isn't it? Did you pick out the colors?"

Maybe Devon had hired a professional decorator....

"Dad fixed it up before we moved in," Jenny said, squashing that theory. "But he asked what my favorite colors were."

Before we moved in.

Caitlin didn't have an opportunity to follow up on the comment, because Jenny grabbed her hand. "Come on. I'll show you my fish."

As they stepped back into the hallway, there was still no sign of Devon.

Jenny ambled down the hall and Caitlin followed her, curious to see the rest of the second floor. "This is where we have school."

The room they entered looked like a cross between a classroom and a playground. Colorful maps decorated the walls and two computer stations flanked the window. An elaborate HO scale train track wound around the entire perimeter of the room, complete with miniature towns and parks.

The dachshund she'd met that first day waddled up to her and Caitlin bent down to scratch the dog's silky ears.

"That's Rosie. Sunny—Josh's iguana—is around here somewhere. She doesn't like to be in her cage. She thinks she's a dog."

Jenny led her around the room like a seasoned tour guide, pointing out the fishbowl and introducing her to Reggie the hamster, another well-fed member of the Walsh household.

They found Sunny sleeping on the top of the bookshelf, but Caitlin kept a polite distance this time, just in case the creature woke up and wanted to compare jewelry again.

Jenny was about to show her the aquarium when Josh and Brady sidled in and flattened themselves against the wall.

"I was admiring the train set," Caitlin said, not quite sure how to engage them in conversation. "Did you put it together yourselves?"

The boys exchanged looks and then, as if coming to some sort of mutual agreement, they both started to talk at once.

"I built the covered bridge." Josh dropped to his knees beside the track. "Watch when it comes through."

"And I wired the lights at the intersections," Brady said, not to be outdone. "It's timed so when the train comes over the bridge, the arm comes down and blocks the road."

Intrigued, Caitlin bent over to get a better look as the train chugged around the track. Just as Brady promised, when the train disappeared inside the bridge, tiny red lights flickered. And the barrier came down to protect the toy cars on the road.

"You guys did this? It's amazing." She meant it.

"We didn't like it at first," Josh whispered. "We thought it was kind of babyish, but dad says trains are something you never outgrow."

Brady shrugged. "Dad sure didn't. He plays with it more than we do."

Caitlin laughed. "He doesn't."

"As a matter of fact," a voice growled behind her. "He does."

Devon would have smiled at the startled look on Caitlin's face. If he hadn't just gotten off the phone with Ashleigh's sister, Vickie.

He'd hoped the two-week silence since her last telephone call meant that her threat to take him to court had been a bluff, but he discovered she'd been using the time to gather ammunition. And the bitter words she'd flung at Devon were still ricocheting around in his head.

"You may have had visitation rights, Devon, but my sister never would have wanted you to raise the children. She wanted them to have all the advantages that she never had, and she knew you weren't able to provide them.

Right before they'd hung up, Vickie had released one final barb: *At least think about Jenny, Devon. A girl needs her mother, and I'm the closest thing she has right now.*

Devon glanced at his daughter and felt a familiar ache spread through his chest.

Was he being selfish? Or was he doing the right thing?

Jenny's eyes met his. "Ms. McBride likes my room, Dad," she said softly.

"She should see ours." Josh and Brady launched to their feet at the same time, as if the movement had been choreographed. "It's better."

Devon was already uneasy that he'd left Caitlin alone again with Jenny while he dealt with Vickie's call. And, he told himself, she was probably anxious to ditch his chaotic household and meet up with her date.

He decided to give her an easy out. "Boys, I already kept Ms. McBride waiting while I took a phone call. Maybe she could see it some other time." If there *was* another time.

"It'll only take two minutes. I'll even time it," Brady said.

"I can take a quick look before we go downstairs." Caitlin's hand rose as if she were about to ruffle his hair, but she quickly withdrew it. "*If* you time it."

The boys gave a loud whoop and stampeded out the door ahead of them.

Caitlin winced. "The two of them can make a lot of noise, can't they?"

"Not usually, but I'm working on it." Devon gave his daughter a playful wink.

Caitlin looked confused, and Jenny giggled.

"Dad says we're too quiet."

"You are. That's why I have to do goofy things like *this*." He took Jenny's hand and twirled her around as if she were Clara in the *Nutcracker*.

"Dad!" Jenny shrieked.

"See, it works every time." Devon released Jenny and she dashed out of the room.

Caitlin shook her head. "My dad used to do that, too."

"Dance with you?"

"Embarrass me."

"I embarrassed her?"

"Absolutely. But don't worry. It goes along with the territory."

Devon groaned. "I'm never going to get this parenting stuff right."

"I doubt that anyone does. I'm not an expert or anything but—"

"Really?" Devon broke in, unable to resist teasing her. "Because I thought I saw that somewhere in the fine print of your contract."

"An expert on *children*." Caitlin shot him an exasperated look. "But from what I've seen—" she repeated the statement "—it looks like there's a lot you're getting right."

Devon stared at her, momentarily speechless, while the warmth of the unexpected compliment spread through him.

He finally found his voice. "Thank you."

"You're welcome."

Only a few feet separated them, but it felt as if the distance between them had shrunk. And the tentative smile they shared felt like a truce. For the first time in a long time, Devon felt as if he had another person on his side. And it felt…good.

"We should—" Caitlin hesitated, as if she wasn't sure what they were supposed to do.

"Go find the kids," Devon said helpfully.

Neither of them moved.

"Dad! Where are you guys?"

Both of them snapped to attention at the sound of Brady's voice.

"On our way," Devon called.

He stepped to the side and Caitlin moved past him, purposefully but still with the graceful, rhythmic sway of a trained dancer.

Somewhere along the line, she'd probably taken walking lessons.

Who are you kidding, Dev? She probably teaches them!

He leaned against the doorframe and kept a safe distance from the mayhem. And from Caitlin.

"You did all this, too?" Caitlin glanced at him over her shoulder.

She didn't have to sound so surprised, Devon thought wryly.

"They'll outgrow it eventually, but I designed the furniture so it can be modified as they get older."

"You *built* the furniture?"

"It's just some lumber and nails pounded together."

"But why—"

"Why what?" Devon prompted.

"Don't most people start with projects that add to the home's resale value? Like redoing the kitchen? Or updating the siding?"

"I'm not most people."

Chapter Ten

Caitlin was beginning to realize that.

And she found herself making an adjustment of her first impression of Devon. Again.

The man was a talented carpenter—so talented she didn't understand why he hadn't pursued it as a career. Wouldn't it generate more of a steady income than writing…*poetry?*

But instead of having the house repainted or the downstairs living area remodeled, he'd chosen to focus his attention on creating a fanciful, comfortable space for his children. One that no one would see during a casual visit to his home.

"Jenny, will you please set the table for dinner? Boys—"

"We know." Two identical sighs blended together. "Take Rosie outside."

The children trooped out, leaving them alone.

"I suppose it's time to go shopping." Devon's tone sounded as long-suffering as the twins'.

"It won't take long. I've got a list of online stores and a pretty good idea, based on the assessment, of what we should order."

"Somehow I knew you would."

Caitlin took that as a compliment.

The next half hour was surprisingly painless. If Caitlin didn't count the way her heart bounced around in her chest like a rubber ball every time Devon's shoulder bumped against hers as they scrolled through the items in the virtual stores on his laptop.

And his proximity didn't do anything to lessen the effects of the aftershock she was still feeling over the moment they'd shared.

She hadn't meant to blurt out the comment about him doing things right, but when she'd seen the combination of regret and doubt move through Devon's eyes, she had to tell him the truth.

He *was* doing a lot of things right.

The quiet gratitude in his simple thank-you had made her glad she'd told him. Even though she'd had the strangest feeling that her words had somehow shifted the boundary of their relationship....

"Are we there yet?"

Devon's plaintive question pulled Caitlin's attention back to the screen. And made her smile.

"Almost." And not a single plaid shirt on the invoices!

Caitlin took a discreet peek at her watch, but Devon caught her.

"You've been here more than an hour. Go ahead. We can finish up another time."

"We're down to shoes and a suit—" Caitlin rushed on to avoid the argument brewing in his eyes. "You can't order a suit online, Devon. It has to be altered to fit."

"I have a suit," he said curtly.

"Oh, but—" Caitlin bit down on her lower lip to prevent the rest of the words from tumbling out. "The styles change—" *From decade to decade.* "Quite rapidly. Do you mind if I take a look at it?"

"Yes, I mind. But since we don't have time for another showdown, I'll try to locate it for inspection."

Devon stalked out of the room and Caitlin slid her notes back into her briefcase. She stood up to stretch her muscles and her foot landed on something soft. When she glanced down, she saw Devon's writing sweater in a heap on the floor.

Caitlin picked it up and smelled the subtle blend of Devon's soap and the unique scent of *him*. She wanted to press it against her nose and inhale…

Instead, she stuffed it into her briefcase.

More than likely, Devon had been joking when he'd told Jenny that he couldn't think unless he was wearing it. She doubted he'd even miss it!

Jenny's head poked out of her room as soon as Caitlin stepped into the hall. "Are you and Dad done?"

"Almost." Caitlin found it easy to smile at the girl. "Do you mind if I borrow your mirror a minute?"

"Okay." Jenny beckoned her into the room and pointed to the oval mirror standing in the corner of her bedroom.

Caitlin took her makeup bag out of her purse and tilted her head several different ways, trying to see her reflection through the rainbow of scarves draped over the glass. "You must not use this one very often," she teased.

Jenny shrugged and Caitlin suddenly remembered the way she'd put her hand over mouth to hide her braces when she'd laughed. With a flash of understanding, Caitlin realized Jenny had covered the mirror on purpose.

Leave it alone, a voice inside her head warned. *Most girls Jenny's age go through a stage when they don't like themselves. And the last time you and Jenny talked, Devon didn't seem too happy about it.*

But as logical as that sounded, Caitlin couldn't prevent the memory that swept her back in time. She could see herself at the age of twelve, curled up on the bed. Not crying, but completely numb.

"When I was your age, some of the girls drew pictures of people in our class. And then they drew arrows to the things

they saw as flaws. Big ears, crooked teeth, that sort of thing."
As she spoke the words, Caitlin's heart contracted a little. As
if she'd pressed her finger against a bruise. "They taped the
pictures on the lunchroom wall and asked people to vote for the
homeliest girl."

"They didn't draw your picture, did they?"

"I won the contest."

Jenny's eyes widened. "But you're...pretty."

"Thank you." Caitlin struck a dramatic pose, pursed her lips
and blew a noisy kiss at the woman in the mirror. A woman who
didn't look anything like the awkward twelve-year-old who'd
once hated everything about herself.

Jenny giggled. "You're funny, too."

"Mmm. Let's keep that between the two of us, shall we?"
Caitlin winked as their eyes met in the mirror.

"The girls at my school teased me, too," Jenny said in a low
voice. "They told me I must be adopted."

Caitlin didn't understand the comment, but she heard the
pain woven into it. She sat down on the bed next to Jenny and
slipped her arm around the girl's slim shoulders, wishing she
possessed Meghan's compassion or Evie's easy rapport with
young people.

"Did you feel...bad? When they drew that picture?"

"Yes." Caitlin exhaled slowly as she allowed another image
to infiltrate her thoughts. Her classmates standing around her
picture, laughing. And the one laughing the loudest had been
the boy she'd had a secret crush on. "But after I talked to my
mom, I wrote an acceptance speech and gave it the next day."

Jenny's shuddered. "Did she...make you?"

"No. But my mom was..." Caitlin's throat tightened. She
hadn't let her thoughts turn back to that conversation in a long
time. "Pretty amazing. She told me that I could either look to
other people to see my reflection and never get a clear picture

of who I was or I could look to God to find out who I am because He's the one who made me. And He loves me. Every part of me—the things I like about myself and the things I'm not so crazy about."

"There are a lot of things I'm not crazy about," Jenny confessed.

Her honest response touched a chord in Caitlin. "I feel the same way sometimes."

"Really?"

"Really. So it's a good thing that the way we feel about ourselves doesn't change the way God feels about us." Another thing Laura McBride had taught her—and another lesson she'd pushed to the back of her mind.

"Dad says the same thing."

Somehow, Caitlin wasn't surprised to hear that. As guarded as Devon was, it was becoming increasingly clear he was a man of integrity. She'd had an inkling of its source, but Jenny's words confirmed it.

"Your dad is right—"

"Those are the kind of words I like to hear." Devon wandered into the bedroom. "What exactly am I right about, by the way?"

Caitlin saw his reflection in the mirror and swallowed hard.

He hadn't simply brought the suit to her for inspection.

He was wearing it.

Devon wasn't expecting to see Caitlin sitting on the bed with her arm around his daughter. And the tip of Jenny's nose was pink—a sure sign she was holding back tears. He gave Caitlin a sharp look.

"Is everything okay?"

"Everything is fine." Caitlin stood up. And she looked almost…guilty. "We were just having a little girl talk."

"Yup. Girl talk," Jenny echoed, sliding off the bed. "I'll set the table now." She paused in the doorway and flashed a winsome smile. "You look great, Dad."

Devon watched her skip out of the room and decided he needed to read another chapter in the book on raising daughters. Otherwise, by the time he figured it out, Jenny would probably have a family of her own.

Caitlin morphed back into the fashion police and prowled around him, studying the suit from all angles.

"Well?" Devon struck a model's pose and tucked his hands into the pockets of his jacket. He hadn't missed Caitlin's skeptical expression when he'd told her that he owned one. Ashleigh had insisted he needed a decent suit if he wanted to accompany her to parties or charity functions. And even though it was almost ten years old, the tailor had assured him it was as classic as a Corvette convertible.

"It's—" Caitlin hesitated.

"Expensive."

"That wasn't what I was going to say," Caitlin murmured.

"Striking?"

"I wasn't going to say that, either."

Devon waited for her to be impressed as she examined the label.

She didn't look impressed. "Did someone…give this to you?"

Devon wondered if he should be offended by the question. Probably. "I *bought* it."

"Well, you're going to need a new one."

"What? Didn't you see the label?"

"Yes, but what does that have to do with anything?"

"I thought that had something to do with everything."

A shadow skimmed through Caitlin's eyes, giving Devon the uneasy feeling he'd said the wrong thing.

"Tell me the truth. Did you *like* to wear this expensive, striking suit?"

She had him there. He'd hated it but he'd been outvoted. He repeated the tailor's mantra. "It's a *classic*."

"You felt like a waiter in it, didn't you?"

"No." He caved in when she raised an eyebrow. "Maybe a penguin," he muttered. "A really *embarrassed* penguin."

"That's because as great as the style is—and no matter whose name is on the label—it isn't *you*. This suit may be a classic, but it's still stuffy and pretentious and you are neither of those things."

His lips twitched. "Thank you. Again."

"You're welcome. Again."

Something danced in the air between them.

Devon broke the silence. For his own good. "Thrift store?"

"Thrift store." Caitlin gathered up her things and didn't bother to check her reflection in the mirror again. "I make several trips a month, so if you can't find the time, I'd be happy to drop it off for you."

Her brisk tone told Devon that it was back to business. He didn't know whether to be relieved or disappointed.

He decided to choose relief. Much less complicated than wondering what she'd feel like in his arms.

"What time are your reservations?" Devon asked. As a ruthless reminder there was a reason Caitlin was wearing that sparkly dress.

"Six-thirty."

Devon frowned. "You're late."

"They'll order without me. I mentioned I had a meeting with a client."

A client. For some reason—one that Devon didn't want to examine too closely—the description stung a little.

What did you expect, he chided himself. *She bent the rules by making a few house calls, but it's not like you're going to see her after she turns you into a socially acceptable guy.*

And it wasn't as if he *wanted* to keep seeing her.

Did he?

The question jump-started another internal argument that continued as Devon followed Caitlin down the stairs. He could only imagine her reaction if he asked her out for dinner.

That's probably the real reason she agreed to come over. So she doesn't have to be seen with you in public. It's time for you to send Caitlin McBride back to her world....

Jenny and the boys rushed up to them.

"Can't you stay for supper, Caitlin?" Jenny blocked their path.

"Ms. McBride," Devon automatically corrected.

"Yeah," Josh chimed in. "Dad's making spaghetti."

"Again," Brady muttered under his breath.

"Guys—don't put Ms. McBride on the spot. You can see she's dressed to—"

"I'd love to stay," Caitlin interrupted, shocking Devon to the core. "I haven't had spaghetti for a long time. And I don't mind if they call me Caitlin."

Devon stared at her. "I thought you were having dinner with friends."

Caitlin smiled at the children. "I am."

Chapter Eleven

"Let me help with that." Caitlin nudged Devon aside as he sawed through a loaf of French bread the size of a small torpedo.

"You aren't exactly dressed to be part of the kitchen crew," he pointed out.

"Do you have an apron?"

He gave her a look. "Please."

"It's perfectly acceptable for the chef to wear an apron, you know."

"You can decide after dinner whether I deserve the title of chef. But since you have that stubborn—you heard me right, I said stubborn—look on your face, just give me a second. I'll be right back."

When Devon returned, he held out one of his shirts.

Caitlin crossed her arms and repeated his word. *"Please."*

"It'll keep your dress clean."

"It's *flannel*." Her eyes narrowed. "Or is it payback?"

"Definitely one. Maybe the other," Devon admitted with a grin. "This is what I used to do when Jenny was little and wanted to help me in the kitchen. Put your arms out," Devon instructed. When she obeyed, he eased the shirt on so it was backward and put his hands on her shoulders to turn her around. "This way, it covers you from your chin down. Trust me. No spaghetti sauce will stain your dress."

Caitlin didn't answer. Because she couldn't. Not with Devon's fingertips skimming the sensitive area near her spine as he buttoned the shirt.

Maybe she shouldn't have stayed.

But when Jenny had invited her for supper, something had happened to Caitlin that she'd barely been able to put a name to.

She'd…waffled.

And the reason she'd waffled wasn't only because she didn't want to extinguish the hopeful look in Jenny's eyes. It was also because she knew exactly what the evening ahead of her would look like and she realized she wasn't looking forward to it.

A late dinner in an upscale restaurant that catered to busy young professionals. The people she planned to meet were more professional acquaintances than friends and the entire conversation would center on work. Who put in the most hours? Who made the most sacrifices?

Caitlin usually won, hands down.

If she were honest with herself, she knew the complaints about jam-packed schedules and long hours weren't really complaints at all. In her social circle, they'd become bragging rights.

But as Caitlin's gaze shifted from Jenny to the boys' eager faces, she'd realized that this type of engagement had begun to leave her increasingly restless. What's more, the witty, sophisticated banter that flew back and forth across the table wasn't nearly as lively as her interactions with Devon's children. Or her verbal sparring matches with Devon.

That insight alone should have had her scrambling for her coat, but Caitlin had surprised herself by accepting Jenny's invitation. And it was clear she'd surprised Devon, too, although he'd been polite enough to mask it.

Caitlin knew he'd accepted her presence to please his children and not because of any burning desire to spend another minute in her company. Maybe they had shared a brief…moment…after she'd complimented his parenting, but that only meant their professional relationship had finally found its footing.

"There. That should work."

"Thank you." Caitlin pushed the words out, relieved to discover her vocal cords weren't permanently damaged.

Devon Walsh seemed to have a knack for throwing off her equilibrium. Which only made her impulsive decision to spend an evening in his company even more confusing.

Caitlin sneaked a glance at the clock. If she left now, she could make it to the restaurant in time to order dessert.…

All three children burst into the kitchen and Jenny laughed when she saw Caitlin's makeshift apron. Only this time, Caitlin noticed, she forgot to cover her braces.

"Okay, everyone listen up," Devon ordered. "Brady, tossed salad. Josh, beverages and, Jenny, dessert."

Caitlin found herself caught in the middle of a sudden flurry of activity. The boys charged around the kitchen while Jenny dumped the ingredients for chocolate pudding into a bowl and turned on the hand mixer.

Listening to their lively conversations—and the occasional argument that broke out—reminded Caitlin so much of her childhood that she felt it like a physical ache.

Ordinarily, she chose *quiet*. She didn't even turn the radio or television on when she was alone in her apartment. So why was her soul soaking up the squeals of laughter and the clanging and crashing of dishes like a dried up loofah?

"Sorry—it's not exactly a well-oiled machine in here, is it?" Devon murmured as he set a bowl of freshly grated parmesan cheese on the counter.

"No." *It was better,* Caitlin thought. But she couldn't tell Devon that because he wouldn't understand.

She wasn't sure if she understood it, either.

She eased away from him. "What else can I do?"

"You can sit down," Devon told her. "As soon as Jenny pours the milk, we're ready to eat."

Caitlin walked over to the table and noticed the piles of books had been relocated to the deacon's bench in the corner and the table set with laminated, handmade placemats. She made an educated guess where Devon would be sitting and chose the chair as far away from it as possible....

"You can't sit there. That chair is for Jesus," Josh said.

Caitlin blinked. "Excuse me?"

"Brady, please get one of the card-table chairs out of the closet, okay?" Devon said hastily. "Go ahead and sit down, Caitlin. Anywhere is fine."

She remained standing, the faintest smile playing at the corners of her lips. "You're going to give Jesus the folding chair?"

"It's not, um, *really* for Jesus. It's more like a…symbol. A reminder. A—"

She took pity on him. Although she wasn't sure why. He *had* made her wear the flannel shirt.

"I understand, Devon," Caitlin interrupted. "My parents did the same thing. My sisters and I had a tendency to turn dinner time into a half-hour long debate session—" Debates that she'd usually orchestrated! "—so the extra chair reminded us to 'make nice.' It made mealtime more peaceful, I suppose."

Like the memory of the conversation with her mother that she'd shared with Jenny, Caitlin hadn't thought about their family tradition of "the unseen dinner guest" in ages.

"So your parents are believers?" Devon was asking.

"Yes—my Dad is, I mean." Caitlin straightened the salt and pepper shakers on the table. "Mom died when I was twenty."

"I'm sorry."

She'd heard the polite words before, usually followed by an awkward pause that Caitlin felt obligated to smooth over. But somehow, the compassionate understanding in Devon's voice was more difficult to dismiss.

And then she felt Jenny's hand on her arm.

"My mom died, too."

Devon softly closed the boys' bedroom door and padded downstairs, expecting to find Caitlin waiting in the foyer. Or already gone.

The boys had had a hard time settling down, stretching out the bedtime routine an extra ten minutes.

No sign of Caitlin.

Disappointment bloomed. What had he expected? It was already past nine o'clock....

He heard a noise coming from the kitchen and followed it.

Caitlin stood at the sink, her back to him as she washed the supper dishes. And without being coerced, bribed or threatened, she'd put on his flannel shirt. Tendrils of glossy dark hair had escaped the elegant twist and feathered the back of her neck.

Maybe, Devon thought as he grabbed a dry towel and silently joined her at the sink, *it would have been better if she'd left.*

She'd spent the entire evening with them. He would have thought she'd be bored to tears but Caitlin had been more than a casual observer of a typical night at the Walsh household— she'd joined right in.

She ate instant pudding out of a chipped bowl and listened while he read the daily chapter in the latest Ransom mystery out loud. After that, she'd kept the children enthralled with a story about her father, who'd discovered the remains of a shipwreck in Lake Superior.

When it came time for bed, she reminded Jenny to wash her face and flipped the nightlight on in the hall for Josh.

And now she was in his kitchen. Washing dishes.

And he was the one who broke the silence.

"Their mother died last May. It's been hard on them."

Caitlin's hands had stilled in the sudsy water. "And on you," she murmured.

Devon didn't answer right away. Six months had gone by and he was still trying to come to terms with Ashleigh's death. Still trying to navigate the channels of his own grief and mixed emotions.

His ex-wife had made some heartbreaking decisions, but Devon had never wished her ill. And he still struggled over the guilt that came from knowing her tragic death had brought his children back into his life.

"We'd been divorced almost seven years," he had finally said carefully. "I'd gotten used to living without her, but knowing I'm not ever going to see her…to hear her voice again…it's difficult."

Caitlin's face tipped toward his and the understanding in her eyes almost undid him. At the moment, it would have been easy to forget that theirs was a business relationship. A *reluctant* business relationship, he reminded himself. The only reason she'd stayed for supper was that Jenny had invited her, not because she'd been eager for a few more hours in his company.

So why, for the first time in years, did he feel an overwhelming urge to share his burdens with someone other than the Lord?

And why did it have to be Caitlin?

"Why do you think their aunt has a chance at getting custody?" she asked. "Wouldn't the original agreement hold up in court?"

A brief silence stretched between them until Devon's sigh stirred the air. "I only had visitation rights. After the divorce, their mother was granted full custody."

"But you must have spent time with them."

Devon's jaw tightened. He couldn't defend himself without giving away too many details but if he told the truth, she was going to think he didn't care about his family. That he hadn't tried hard enough. Sometimes he wondered if it were true. "I can count the number of times on one hand I saw them after the divorce was final."

Caitlin's forehead wrinkled. "But what about summer? Breaks during the school year?"

"I tried to have the custody ruling overturned several times. I'd started fixing up the house but eventually even my lawyer told me that we were fighting a losing battle. He advised me to be patient until the kids were old enough to make their own decisions."

Devon braced himself to see the look of doubt, or worse yet, judgment, in her eyes. Instead, the compassion that warmed Caitlin's blue eyes nearly undid him.

"I'm sorry."

How could she communicate so much with so few words, Devon wondered.

"The only thing that kept me going was finding a Gideon Bible in the hotel room I'd rented." A glimmer of wry humor lit his eyes at the memory. "There was cable in the room, but, as usual, nothing worth watching. I pulled out the Bible and saw a bookmark stuck in it. Out of idle curiosity, I opened it up. The person had underlined John 3:16. I read it and kept going. It wasn't until I came to another verse, thirteen chapters later, that I was ready to accept what I was reading as truth."

Devon glanced at Caitlin, wondering if he was boring her. But once he'd started retelling the story, he found he couldn't stop.

"I came to the verse where Jesus said, 'I have told you these things, so that in me you may have peace. In this world you will have trouble. But take heart. I have overcome the world.'" Devon quoted the passage from memory. "I think at that moment, given what was happening in my life, if I'd read a verse that said life would be a breeze if I believed what God said, I would have put the Bible back in the drawer and turned on ESPN. But Jesus got to me. He was honest. Trouble, hard times, they're a reality. But He promised I would find peace in Him. And I did."

Peace.

Caitlin could honestly say she wasn't familiar with the feeling. There were times she tried to cultivate it by going to the spa or taking a jog through the park, but it had always remained elusively out of reach.

And she wasn't sure why.

It wasn't, Caitlin thought a little defensively, as if she didn't believe in God. She'd given her life to Christ while still in elementary school. But life had gotten so busy after she'd graduated from college and decided to take a risk and start her own business.

She had a promise to keep and that promise had kept her focused and single-minded.

Maybe she hadn't walked away from her faith as much as she'd checked it like a coat. Planning to retrieve it at a more convenient time. But she'd never felt as if she were missing something...until now. Until Devon's simple story was like a spotlight aimed at her heart—it lit up the empty corners of her heart. Made her aware of things that were missing.

"I'm sorry." Devon slanted a rueful look in her direction. "You didn't exactly sign up for a sermon with KP."

He'd mistaken her silence for judgment. When really, it stemmed from the knowledge that she'd misjudged him.

Caitlin had listened while he'd carefully answered her questions about the custody issue, refusing to cast blame or make excuses. The things he *hadn't* said made her respect him all the more.

And she had no doubt that he loved his children. She saw it

in his smile. In the twin beds meticulously crafted to resemble pirate ships. The colors he'd chosen for Jenny's room. She'd seen it at supper when he'd led them in prayer and later in his unwavering patience during the bedtime rituals.

She'd never met anyone like Devon before—his casual disregard for convention confused her. His strength and sensitivity tugged at her like a magnetic field. It was the reason she'd stayed.

But it was also the reason she had to leave.

Chapter Twelve

Devon pressed his forehead against the window, watching the headlights fade as Caitlin's Mini Cooper cruised down the street and disappeared around the corner.

His sigh fogged a circle on the glass.

Maybe you could explain this to me, God.

He hadn't even dated since the divorce. Trust didn't come easily for him anymore, and yet he'd come close to baring his soul. To an ambitious businesswoman with connections that had the potential to shine a spotlight on his privacy.

You weren't the only one who let their guard down tonight.

Devon brushed the thought aside but couldn't dispel the images that accompanied it.

Images of Caitlin. Sitting prim and proper at the dinner table—and then curling up on the old velvet sofa, her feet tucked underneath her. Cuddling Rosie against her sparkly designer dress. Patiently answering the boys' questions about the treasure her father had found.

She surprised him at every turn. Cool and caustic with him one moment and the next, there'd be a hint of vulnerability in her smile or a glimpse of warm affection in her eyes when she watched the children's lively antics.

And the way they responded to her was nothing short of astonishing. People at New Hope Fellowship tried to draw the children out but they hadn't met with much success.

Not as effortlessly as Caitlin did. She didn't even seem to try.

Devon turned away from the window, as if a change in location would change the direction of his thoughts.

He already regretted the little he'd told her about Ashleigh. After she'd walked out on him, she'd legally changed her name from Walsh to Heath, her maiden name, but it wouldn't be difficult for a tenacious person to do a little amateur detective work and begin to connect the dots.

And Caitlin was definitely tenacious.

Devon caught himself smiling and scrubbed it away with the back of his hand.

Her abrupt departure had said more than her silence after he'd shared the starting point in his relationship with Christ.

When she'd told him about her parents, he'd assumed she was a believer, too.

I don't know what I'm thinking, Lord. It's too risky. After tonight, I'm done with Caitlin McBride. I...we...don't need her.

The unexpected answer came back just as swiftly.

Maybe she needs you.

"Ms. McBride? There's a Jennifer Walsh on the line."

Caitlin, who had just hung up from a call with Dawn at *Twin City Trends*, snatched it up again. Completely forgetting she'd made a decision that her relationship with the Walsh family could no longer extend beyond her consultations with Devon. Her very *brief* consultations with Devon. Hopefully conducted over the telephone.

"Jenny? This is Caitlin."

Silence.

Caitlin's heart stumbled. "Is everything all right?"

"I think so...but can you come over?"

Caitlin hesitated. When Devon had cracked open the door of his personal life while they'd washed dishes together a few nights ago, she hadn't been tempted to turn and run in the opposite direction like she had in the past. Whenever someone wanted to get close to her, Caitlin instinctively backed away.

But not with Devon. Oh, no. With Devon, just the opposite had occurred. She'd wanted to know more about him. She'd wanted to know *everything* about him.

And that had rattled her more than the sight of his biceps in his sawn off T-shirt or the touch of his hands against her back when he'd buttoned up the flannel shirt.

"You want me to come over?" Caitlin repeated, stalling. "Isn't your dad there?"

"Dad went to get his hair cut."

The quaver in Jenny's voice cut right to Caitlin's heart. "You're alone?"

"I'm old enough to babysit," Jenny said quickly. "But there's a man hanging around...Brady and Josh have been spying on him for a while and they think he's taking pictures."

Caitlin was already reaching for her purse. "I'll be right over."

Sabrina's mouth fell open as she charged through the reception area. "Where are you—"

"Emergency meeting." Caitlin sent up a prayer that it *wasn't* an emergency.

"But what about Mrs. Butter—"

"Reschedule our appointment and set up a complimentary facial at the spa. Please."

The door snapped shut behind her and Caitlin sprinted to her car.

The traffic lights cooperated and as she turned the car onto

Devon's street, she saw a man lingering near the corner of the property, half-hidden by the willow tree bowing over the fence. And the boys were right. He did have a camera.

The sound of her car door closing alerted him and before Caitlin had a chance to question him, he jumped into an SUV with tinted windows and drove away.

She didn't even have a chance to jot down the license plate number.

By the time she reached the gate, Jenny stood on the other side, waiting for her.

"Did he come up to the door?"

Jenny shook her head. "The gate was locked."

Caitlin wrapped her arm around the shivering girl and scowled after the retreating SUV. "Is your dad home yet?"

"Not yet. I have his cell phone number but he didn't answer it."

Caitlin knew that in a roundabout way, that was probably her fault. If Devon had gone to the salon she'd recommended, Valeria, the stylist, collected all her customer's cell phones and PDA's at the door so she wouldn't be interrupted.

"I'll stay here until he gets back." The relief on Jenny's face blurred the fine print in Caitlin's contract. "Do you have any idea who he was? Have you seen him before?"

"No. We were playing hide-and-seek, and Josh spotted him sneaking around."

"Is he gone?" Josh eased out from behind a tree and Brady popped out of the center of a nearby shrub.

"He's gone." Caitlin tried to hide her concern. "I told Jenny I'd stay for a little while if that's okay with you."

"You can play hide-and-seek with us," Brady said.

"Oh, I don't—" Caitlin relented at their eager expressions. "All right. For a few minutes."

"I'll be it." Josh offered.

"You have to count to fifty," Brady said. "I'll let you use my stopwatch."

"And no peeking," Jenny added.

Josh scowled as he walked toward the steps. "I *never* peek."

Jenny and Brady huddled together—obviously choosing a hiding spot was a corporate effort—and then Jenny whispered a few suggestions to Caitlin.

She chose the one that didn't involve crouching, climbing or crawling under something. Which led her to the dilapidated old tool shed near the back of the house.

"Twenty-one. Twenty-two." There was a sudden break in Josh's counting before he started up again.

The game stirred up Caitlin's natural love of competition and when the shed door opened with a soft creak, she felt a stab of disappointment at being discovered so quickly.

"Caitlin?"

Caitlin stifled a groan. Josh hadn't found her.

Devon had.

"Josh said you were in here." Devon eased the door shut behind him, still not quite convinced that the woman crouched down behind the rusty old bicycle wasn't a figment of his imagination.

"But he's still counting!" Caitlin frowned. "How did he know where I was?"

Devon shrugged, not trusting his voice at the moment. "He peeks."

"I should have known. Meghan did the same thing when she was it." Caitlin stepped out of the gloom, daintily picking cobwebs off her coat sleeve. In a plaid skirt, a sweater the color of lemon sorbet and ankle-high leather boots, Caitlin looked as out of place in the dreary shed as she had in his kitchen.

As she would in his life.

This is getting ridiculous, Devon thought. He hadn't talked to Caitlin or seen her for almost a week, but the sight of her still had the power to send his pulse into overdrive. What was worse was the sudden realization that the case of writer's block he'd been suffering from was *her* fault.

He'd missed her dry wit and the way her lips pursed when she was deep in thought. Or softened when she watched his children interact. He'd missed having her to tease and spar with.

He'd missed *her*.

Devon wouldn't let his thoughts go too far down that path. Hadn't he learned his lesson the first time around?

Ashleigh had wanted more than he could provide for her and their children. She'd wanted more than *him*.

He'd naively thought they valued the same things, that loving each other and raising their children together were top priorities. But Ashleigh had eventually lost her respect for him, misinterpreting his contentment with their life as a lack of ambition.

Why would Caitlin be any different? She made no secret of the fact that her career came first.

"Why are you here?" he blurted.

"Jenny. The boys saw a man hanging around." She hesitated for a moment. "Taking pictures."

Dread chilled Devon's blood. "Did you see him?"

"He drove away before I had a chance to talk to him. Jenny couldn't get in touch with you so she called…me."

"Was it possible the guy was a Realtor? Taking pictures of the house next door?" Devon knew he was grasping at straws but didn't want to consider the alternative.

"It's possible." Doubt weighted Caitlin's tone. "He had a camera but I didn't actually see him taking pictures. Who do you think it was?"

A reporter?

Devon bit back the first words that came to mind. More than likely, the stranger had something to do with the summons he'd received the day before, formally requesting his presence in family court the week before Christmas. Vickie had started the proceedings.

Guilt gnawed at the edges of his thoughts. He shouldn't have left the children alone—not even for a few hours—but the summons had spurred him into calling the number on the business card Caitlin had given him to schedule a haircut.

Unfortunately, the stylist named Valeria had dissolved into a fit of laughter when he'd called after breakfast, asking if he could get a haircut. He'd gone to a nearby, old-fashioned barber shop instead. A quarter of the cost and half the time, not that it mattered. He still hadn't been there when his children needed him....

"Devon?" Hesitantly, as if she wasn't sure whether she should follow through on the impulse or not, Caitlin reached out her hand and touched his arm.

The concern in her gaze plowed through Devon's defenses like a wrecking ball. Before he remembered he didn't talk about his personal business, the truth spilled out. "He was probably the private investigator my sister-in-law hired to prove that the house is falling down around our ears. Which might lead a judge to the conclusion that I'm as lax about parenting as I am about home improvements."

"You aren't lax about either one," Caitlin murmured. "It doesn't seem fair to judge the outside of the house and not take into consideration what you've done on the inside."

It sounded good in theory, but Ashleigh's lawyer had dissected his life six years ago, making it look as if he had nothing substantial or valuable to offer his children.

And he'd lost them.

"I'm surprised you have a problem with that, considering what you do for a living." Pain welled up inside of Devon and escaped like steam from a boiler valve. And Caitlin happened to be standing in the blast zone.

Her hand fell away. "What do you mean?"

"Isn't that what you do? Slap a fresh coat of paint on the outside of a person, so to speak? Manipulate their image so they can hide who—or what—they are on the inside?"

The concern fled from her eyes, replaced once again by the cool, distant businesswoman. She moved away from him. "You're right. That's exactly what I do. And now that you're here, I should get back to it."

Devon felt two inches tall. She'd given up a Saturday afternoon to make a house call, scheduled evening appointments to help him order clothes and today she'd taken the time to answer his daughter's call for help. It wasn't fair to take out his frustration on her.

He scraped a hand through his hair. His much *shorter* hair. "I'm sorry, Cait. I get a little unglued when it comes to my kids. I guess I need to brush up on my social graces." It was a flimsy apology, not strong enough to heal the flash of hurt he'd seen in her eyes before she'd looked away. He took a deep breath and a very big risk. "And when it comes to trusting people—I admit I'm a little...rusty."

So am I, Caitlin thought.

But she couldn't say the words out loud. Somehow, they'd gotten lodged under the lump that had formed in her throat, compliments of Devon's gruff apology.

How was she supposed to keep her professional boundaries in place when Devon refused to play by the rules? When he was...honest?

This was the second time he'd let his guard down and shared a piece of his life but Caitlin wasn't flattered. She was terrified. In all of her relationships—business and personal—she set the tone. She determined the boundaries. Her father, Evie and Meghan were the only ones who blithely disregarded them. They cheerfully tromped into her personal space without a second thought. They saw her at her best and at her worst—and they loved her anyway.

And she fiercely loved them back.

But that's what you've been looking for, isn't it? The question slipped into her thoughts before she could stop it. *Someone who knows everything about you and loves you not in spite of it, but because of it?*

I'm not looking for anyone, Caitlin argued back. *I have a plan—and it doesn't include Devon Walsh.*

"Cait? Did you hear me? I'm sorry."

"If you were really sorry, you'll stop calling me *Cait*," she muttered. Not that she really minded. Not many people—only her family—had shortened her name before and it made her feel kind of…special.

Special.

Caitlin decided it was time to go. But before she could move, Devon reached up to brush a strand of hair off her cheek.

"I do…appreciate you stopping by to check on things. Thank you."

Caitlin felt the weight of his worry over the children as if he'd somehow transferred it to her through that simple touch.

She sensed Devon was waiting for something. That she didn't know what it might be only convinced her even more that she was better at recognizing what colors looked best on her than she was at recognizing her own emotions.

Devon's eyes softened with understanding. "Caitlin, I—"

The door of the shed flew open and Brady rushed in. "Hey, Dad! I found something cool. Come on."

Chapter Thirteen

The boy grabbed his father's arm and towed him outside. Caitlin would have chosen that moment to make her escape but Brady glanced over his shoulder. "Aren't you coming, Caitlin?"

She tried to squash the tiny spark of pleasure she felt at being included, knowing that Devon's children weren't drawn to her personally. They missed their mother, she reasoned. They'd be drawn to any woman who showed them attention.

But Caitlin still couldn't walk away from the appeal in those big brown eyes.

"I suppose I am." If she could get her legs to move. Her ankles felt like jelly inside her boots.

What had Devon been about to say? And why had he touched her? Her cheek still felt warm from the gentle brush of his fingertips.

Caitlin was careful to keep her distance from Devon as they trudged into the backyard. Brady darted toward the enormous willow tree, where Jenny and Josh waited.

"We think it's a diamond!" Josh shouted, jumping up and down.

"I found it when I was hiding," Brady explained before charging ahead of them.

"They must be pretending they're Matt and Marty Ransom again," Devon said under his breath. "Yesterday they were convinced that an old painting they found in the basement had to be a stolen Da Vinci."

Caitlin struggled to match his casual tone, not wanting him to see how much their conversation had affected her. "You should stop reading those mysteries. They've even got *me* looking sideways at the doorman. I'd never noticed his shifty eyes before."

"No kidding." Devon slanted a glance at her. "So you're a D. Birch fan now?"

"Your kids have gotten me hooked. I'm thinking about buying the series for Christmas. My sister's husband, Sam, has a niece about Jenny's age who might enjoy them. Josh mentioned the fourth book is coming out right before Christmas."

"December fourteenth."

Caitlin shook her head. "You know the exact release date? Are you planning to stand in line at midnight for a signed copy or something?"

"Not exactly," Devon muttered.

"Hurry up!" Brady howled.

"This is probably worth a million dollars." Josh's eyes glowed with excitement. "Maybe a billion."

"It's taken me all summer to get these boys to loosen up and enjoy life a little," Devon whispered. "Play along."

Caitlin gulped. "How am I supposed to do that?"

"Use your imagination."

"Meghan says I don't have one."

"It's in there somewhere. And you have five seconds to find it."

It was a good thing, Caitlin decided, that she worked well under pressure. Especially if a deadline was involved.

As they stepped around the tree, Caitlin saw a large heart cut into the bark. Two letters had been carved inside of it.

Jenny's face was as animated as her brothers' as she pointed to a deep indentation in the trunk. "Right here. See, it's wedged in this hole."

While Devon leaned closer for a better look, Caitlin tried to figure out the best way to play along. Growing up, she'd preferred games that required skill instead of imagination but there were times she hadn't been able to escape Evie's pitiful plea for her to play "school." She gave in on the condition that she could be the principal.

"It has to be fake," Devon said cautiously.

Caitlin frowned. It didn't sound as if Devon were playing along to her. She inched closer to see what he was looking at and sucked in a breath.

Something shiny *was* winking in the hole underneath the initials. And it did look suspiciously like a…diamond. Devon must have planted it there on purpose, hoping his sons would find it. It made sense, considering he'd been encouraging their dual identities as the Ransom brothers.

"Do you have your pocketknife, Dad?" Jenny asked.

Devon patted down the pockets of his blue jeans. "Sorry."

Caitlin smiled in satisfaction. *Now* she could play along.

"I might have something." She opened her purse and fished around inside of it until her fingers closed around a tiny plastic case. "Here. Try these."

Devon cocked an eyebrow at the tweezers she put in his palm. "Are you a Girl Scout?"

"That would be my sister, Evie. Always prepared for any emergency," Caitlin said wryly. "Me? I'm the one prepared for any *fashion* emergency."

"We all have our gifts." The look Devon sent in her direction made Caitlin forget that her toes had gone numb from the cold while she'd been hiding in the shed.

Everyone crowded around Devon as he carefully scraped at the soft bark around the "diamond." It almost looked as if the trunk had grown around it and it wasn't recently poked into the hiding place.

"Can we keep it?" Brady whispered.

"Yeah, finders keepers," Josh said.

"I'm afraid this thing is too big to be real, guys." Devon finally worked the gem free.

As everyone crowded around, Caitlin tried to focus on the piece of jewelry cradled in Devon's palm instead of his lean, well-shaped hand.

The ring boasted an exquisite marquis-cut diamond set off to perfection on an ornate band of what looked to be…

"Gold."

She must have said it out loud, because everyone turned to stare at her.

"I told you!" Brady whooped. "It's real."

Devon was looking at her as if he'd forgotten that he'd been the one to tell her to play along in the first place.

"I don't think so. If it was, it would be worth a small fortune."

"Look at the setting," Caitlin pointed out. "It's got to be an antique. And the band isn't exactly the adjustable kind."

"It might have been expensive but that doesn't mean it's real," Devon pointed out.

"Do you mind if I take a closer look?"

Devon shrugged and dropped the ring in her hand. Caitlin scraped off some of the grime with her thumbnail and held the ring up to better capture the light. The bright fire that flashed off the multifaceted stone told her there was a good chance the diamond was authentic.

She looked up at Devon. "Who lived here before you?"

"I have no idea. The house was a foreclosure so I bought it from the bank. From what I understand, it sat empty for four or five years, waiting for someone crazy enough to want a fixer-upper."

"You mean someone *committed* enough, don't you?" Caitlin corrected.

"The loan officer did use that word," Devon mused. "Although in a slightly different context."

"Do you think it belongs to the people who carved their initials in the tree?" Jenny asked.

"It doesn't belong to them anymore," Brady muttered.

"Judging from the size, it has to be close to a full carat," Devon said. "I don't think someone would hide something that valuable in a tree—"

"It's engraved." Caitlin didn't mean to interrupt but when she wiped the ring off, she'd caught a glimpse of an inscription on the inside of the band.

"Let me see that," Devon demanded.

"Please," Jenny coached her father under her breath.

Caitlin hid a smile at Devon's disgruntled look. *"Please."* He squinted at the tiny, flowing script inside the band: 1 Cor. 13:7.

"It's a secret message," Brady breathed.

"It's a message, all right, but not exactly a secret one. It's in the Bible," Devon explained patiently.

"How are we going to find out who it belongs to?" Jenny asked, eyes wide with concern.

"I have an idea." Josh's eyes began to sparkle. "Ms. McBride's dad can help. He's a treasure hunter."

Caitlin took a step back. "He's not really a treasure hunter. He finds…lost things for people."

"Maybe this time he could find a person for a lost thing," Brady said.

The logic of children.

Caitlin tried to find a gracious way to wiggle out of involving Patrick McBride.

"My dad lives a long way away. I don't think he could do much—"

"But you said he uses the Internet a lot," Josh reminded her.

"We could help him, too," Brady added. "I have my own e-mail address and everything."

"We'd be like Matt and Marty Ransom but this time we won't be pretending." Josh looked at his brother and the boys slapped their palms together and then added a chest bump for good measure.

"Your dad is right." Caitlin tried to backpedal. "The diamond might not be real."

"We can take it to the jewelry store and ask, can't we, Dad?" Jenny asked.

"I…suppose."

"And then Ms. McBride's dad can help us find out who put it there."

Three pairs of hopeful eyes turned toward her.

Caitlin tried to convince herself that involving her father was the logical solution. He did have the time. And the connections.

Patrick didn't have to know anything about the Walsh family—and Devon in particular—other than that they needed his help, did he?

No, he didn't.

And it didn't mean she had to spend any more time with Devon once she made the initial introductions did she?

No, she didn't.

"All right. I'll call him when I get home." She'd introduce them—via the World Wide Web—and step back.

All her father would have to know was that one of her clients needed help that didn't involve a skin analysis or a personal image profile.

* * *

"You didn't tell us that you'd hired Dad to help your friend Devon!"

Caitlin counted to five and then tacked on a few more numbers for good measure. Because this time, it was Evie, not Meghan, on the phone. Proof that a grapevine didn't have to be large to be effective!

And how was it that Meghan, who couldn't remember important things like changing the registration sticker on her license plate or filing her taxes on time, had remembered Devon's first name? And passed the information onto Evie?

She should have known her nosy sisters would get wind of her phone call to their father.

After Josh and Brady had called her—at work, on speaker phone—to let her know the diamond was, in fact, genuine, Caitlin had tried her best to stay out of the situation. It was hard not to let their excitement over a real-live mystery reel her in but she'd managed to. Even though it had meant squeezing in a few more clients after the regular workday and scheduling extra shopping hours with Margaret Peterson, the woman who'd won the makeover contest.

"Mr. Walsh is a *client*."

Her statement fell upon deaf ears.

"Dad mentioned he has three children?" Evie posed it as a question; although Caitlin had a hunch her sister already knew those alleged children's names and birth dates!

"Yes, he does."

"Dad said that Brady found a diamond ring stuck in a tree. Right underneath some initials."

Brady. Uh-huh. She was right. Evie did know their names.

"I'll bet his wife hopes no one steps forward to claim the ring."

Caitlin rolled her eyes. *Pitiful.* Evie might have successfully dodged a corrupt group of treasure hunters the summer before but she still needed a few more lessons in order to earn her spy badge.

"Dev—*Mr. Walsh*…is single."

"Single. Really." A thoughtful pause followed and Caitlin braced herself for round two of the inquisition. "It couldn't have been much of a ring if someone discarded it so easily."

Caitlin remembered the white fire caught and reflected in the strategically cut facets. "It's beautiful."

"You saw it?"

"I was there when—" Ack! She'd stumbled right into her sister's trap. Maybe Evie *had* earned her spy badge! "I was at their house on business, that's all. I had to check on…something."

The children, not that she needed to mention that particular detail to her meddling sibling!

Caitlin heard a muffled giggle in the background. A muffled giggle that sounded suspiciously like Meghan.

She should have known.

"We're not in junior high anymore," Caitlin said sourly. "You two don't have to sneak around now and look for my diary."

"Do you still keep a diary?" Evie asked.

"It's been replaced by her BlackBerry." The muffled whisper wasn't as muffled this time.

"Hi, Meghan."

"Meghan?" Evie sounded innocently confused. "This is Evie."

"I thought you both had matured beyond the tormenting-the-oldest-sister game."

"Oh, some things a person never outgrows. They're much too entertaining," Meghan interjected cheerfully.

"I knew it," Caitlin muttered.

Mr. Darcy, who'd been curled up at her feet, suddenly stirred. He jumped down from the sofa and made a beeline for the door, his tail sweeping back and forth through the air like a furry—albeit crooked—windshield wiper.

At least now she'd have an excuse to cut the conversation short!

"It was great of you to ask Dad for help," Evie said seriously. "He's pretty excited. He's already bonding with the twins. They e-mail him every day for updates."

Evie knew the boys were twins? Wait a second, had she used the word *bonding*.

No! Caitlin silently howled. *There should be no bonding!* She'd been doing her best to stay away from the Walshes.

And it's been working so well for you, hasn't it? Caitlin ignored the mocking voice in her head.

"Dad invited Devon and the kids to take a field trip up to Superior in the spring. I'm thinking about meeting them there to show them some of the waterfalls and limestone caves."

"The last time you took someone on a field trip, you ended up running for your life from some scary psycho-goon," Caitlin reminded her between gritted teeth.

"But she scared him off with a homemade bomb." Pride tinged Meghan's voice.

"It wasn't a bomb, it was a distraction," Evie corrected her sister primly. "And just for the record, I've gone on several field trips since then without a scary psycho-goon in sight…or the need to practice a field experiment," she added for good measure.

Talking to her sisters, Caitlin decided, was like being caught in a blender. She tried to change to subject. "So what's new with you?"

"I don't have any new clients," Meghan said.

Caitlin stabbed her knitting needle into the unsuspecting ball of yarn at her side. "Evie?"

"I don't have any new clients, either." Laughter thickened the words. "But I have two new students."

"In the middle of a semester?"

"They were MK's. You know, missionary kids. Their mom homeschooled them until they came back to the States recently."

"Homeschooled?" Meghan repeated. "Wow. That's really a commitment. Don't you think so, Caitlin?"

"Definitely a commitment."

Were there no secrets?

"Okay, Lucy and Ethel." Caitlin launched to her feet. "It's been fun but Mr. Darcy is waiting patiently to go outside now for afternoon chipmunk surveillance. Bye!"

"Aren't you on your cell?" Meghan asked suspiciously. "Why can't you just carry the phone with you and keep talking to us?"

Absolutely not.

"Have to go now. Take care. Miss you—"

"Do you really miss us?" Meghan interrupted.

"I do miss you...I can't wait to see you again."

"How sweet. Isn't that sweet, Meghan?"

"Sweet," Meghan agreed.

A sense of foreboding struck Caitlin as it occurred to her that the phone didn't sound the same way it usually did when they were on a conference call. The line sounded much more...clear.

"Why is that sweet?" She had to ask.

"Because we happen to be standing right outside your door!"

It wasn't possible.

Caitlin yanked the door open. Her sisters stood in the hall, both of them almost doubled over with laughter.

"Intervention!" they chorused.

"Oh, really. And just what is it that you're saving me from?"

Her sisters exchanged knowing looks. And then they each tucked an arm through hers. So she couldn't escape.

"We're saving you from yourself," Meghan announced.

Chapter Fourteen

Caitlin took a leisurely sip of coffee and double-checked the calendar on her laptop, even though she knew she would see the wonderful words *Personal Day* written there.

The coffee took a sudden, swift detour into her lungs. Her entire morning had been blocked off with one word: Appointment.

Caitlin snatched up the phone and punched in the number on speed dial that connected her to the office.

"IMAGEine. This is—"

"It's Caitlin."

"Oh, good morning, Ms. McBride."

"Good morning." Caitlin pushed the words out. "Why do I have appointments scheduled this morning? On my day off." Her *one* day off. The day off she'd planned to use to sort through and categorize her tangled emotions over a certain poet. And to recover from her sisters' intervention—the one that had really been more like an ambush!

"It's only one appointment. And you said if there was ever an emergency you would schedule a client on your day off, didn't you?"

Caitlin rubbed her temples. "Yes, I did say that. All right, that brings me to the next question...." She waited.

"Your, um, next question?"

"What *is* the emergency, Sabrina?"

"Oh. Of course. Mr. Walsh needed a personal shopper. And *he* used the word emergency."

Obviously Devon and his awesome cheekbones could move mountains. And ordinarily immovable assistants.

"Please call Mr. Walsh and tell him that I am unavailable to accompany him this morning."

"I can't call him. I think he's already—"

The doorbell rang and Mr. Darcy flicked a curious glance at her from his comfortable post on the arm of the sofa.

"Don't look at me," Caitlin muttered. "I have no idea who—" But suddenly, she did. *"Sabrina."*

"—on his way over," Sabrina finished timidly.

"You gave him my home address?" Caitlin hissed.

Maybe she could pretend she wasn't here...

"Cait? It's Devon. I know you're in there. I heard you talking."

Somehow, he'd sneaked past the security key pad in the foyer.

"I'll fire you later, Sabrina," Caitlin growled into her cell.

"Yes, Ms. McBride." The amusement in her assistant's voice made Caitlin wonder what was happening to her familiar world. She snapped the phone shut, marched over to the door and flung it open.

"You need a personal shopper. Today. I never set up a shopping appointment with a client on the spur of the moment. These things take—"

"Planning, I know." Devon grinned as he sauntered past her. "That's why I planned it."

"*You* planned it," Caitlin sputtered.

"I did. So let's go."

"Do I look like I'm ready to go?" Caitlin suddenly remembered she'd dressed for "veggie" day. The one day of the month she stayed home, lounging around in a T-shirt and the sweatpants she'd had since college. She'd tied her hair back with a tie-dyed scarf Meghan had given to her as a joke on her last birthday and put on—*oh, please no*—Devon's "lucky" writing sweater.

This was worse than being caught in her stocking feet. She'd put Devon's sweater in the thrift store pile but right before she'd unloaded the items from the trunk of her car, in a moment of temporary insanity, she'd plucked it out of the box.

It was…comfortable. And it smelled good. And who knew? Maybe suede elbow patches would make a comeback.…

"Actually, you look great." Devon's gaze flickered over her and his eyes narrowed. "Nice sweater, by the way. Very, what's the word I'm looking for—*retro?*"

His smile curled her toes.

"Hopelessly outdated." Why was she smiling back? "Give me one good reason why I should go shopping with you today?"

"Because I'm not here today as a client. Today I'm here as a friend. And this friend needs your help."

A friend.

What was she supposed to say to that?

"Give me five minutes to change into something more presentable." That's what she said.

After Caitlin disappeared, Devon wandered around the apartment, looking for clues that would give him more insight into the woman wearing the designer dress who'd sat at his table, eating spaghetti, on a folding chair. The one who'd managed to bring a smile to his daughter's face and agreed to help his sons solve the mystery behind the ring they'd found.

The one who'd been dodging his phone calls all week.

Devon recognized survival tactics. He'd perfected an entire

repertoire of his own. But no matter how hard he tried, he hadn't been able to get Caitlin out of his mind. Or out from under his skin.

He'd been married for six years but he had no frame of reference for the feelings that Caitlin stirred inside of him.

Ashleigh had been his first love. Their romance had blossomed during their sophomore year of high school. Devon couldn't believe it when she'd noticed him. Beautiful but capricious, Ashleigh turned his world upside down. The differences in their personalities sparked more fireworks than the Fourth of July, but Devon naively thought they made the relationship more interesting. Devon assumed his young wife was as content as he was.

It wasn't until after the divorce, when Devon had done some soul searching, that he began to wonder if Ashleigh's desire to marry him had been more about breaking away from her own unhappy home life than the desire to build a home of her own.

It had been tough to swallow, knowing she'd used him as an escape route. And even tougher to accept that he might have done the same thing.

Ashleigh hadn't been the only one who'd wanted a fresh start. He hadn't had the most idyllic childhood, either. As the son of a man more devoted to a bottle than his family, Devon had wanted to prove to everyone that he wasn't like his father. And what better way to accomplish that goal than to marry his high school sweetheart, get a respectable job and create a stable home for their family?

He'd been committed to their marriage vows until Ashleigh left, but he wondered if they'd both mistaken infatuation for love.

He wasn't sure anymore *what* love was supposed to look like. Or feel like.

The only thing Devon knew for sure was that God had to be the foundation a relationship was built on in order for it to last.

Which brought him back to his disconcerting feelings for Caitlin.

She'd mentioned that her parents had been believers but hadn't said what *she* believed.

He hadn't been able to forget the "still, small voice" he'd heard the night she'd stayed for dinner, telling him that Caitlin needed them.

Impossible though that seemed.

Look around, Dev. His own doubts clamored for attention. *It doesn't look like you can compete with what she already has.*

Devon padded over to the window. Naturally, the view was phenomenal. A grounds crew probably worked 24-7 to make sure no dead leaves collected on the lawn.

The furniture was simple, elegant and covered in ivory leather—a tempting canvas for juvenile graffiti. There wasn't a single crayon drawing among the original artwork on the walls.

The only thing that seemed out of place was the cat who kept winding around his legs, trying to trip him as he explored.

Devon wasn't surprised Caitlin had a pet; what surprised him was the pet she *had*. Somehow, he'd have guessed she would have chosen one of those pricey little designer dogs she could tote around in a Gucci bag, not a crooked-tailed cat with the tips of both ears missing.

"Hey." Devon bent down and fingered the tag hanging off the preppy-looking collar. "She got to you, too, didn't she, buddy?"

"I'm ready." Caitlin sounded a little breathless as she hurried up behind him.

"No rush. I'm just getting acquainted with…Mr. Darcy." Devon grinned.

Color tinted Caitlin's cheeks. "He doesn't usually like strangers."

"We bonded over a mutual dislike for argyle. But I have to tell you that considering his name, I'm surprised you don't have him wearing a cravat."

Caitlin laughed. "It's at the dry cleaners. Now, could we please go before I change my mind?"

At the moment, Devon found that he couldn't go anywhere. Not with his feet stuck to the floor. It was only the second time he'd heard her laugh like that but the impact was the same. A two-by-four smack to the solar plexus.

"Where are we going by the way? Shoe shopping? The men's department to find a suit? A new pair of shoes?"

Confession time. "The grocery store."

"Why are we going to the grocery store?"

"Because I'm making Thanksgiving dinner next week, and I have no idea what I'm doing."

"How many people will be there for dinner?" Caitlin watched Devon balance an enormous frozen turkey on top of all the other items in the shopping cart.

"It depends," Devon murmured distractedly. "Are you sure we have enough stuffing mix? Because I don't think that little bag of croutons is going to fill this guy up."

Caitlin suppressed a smile. "The stuffing fluffs up as it cooks."

"Oh. Right." He shook his head. "I'm beginning to think that shopping for a pair of shoes might be easier. What else do we need?"

Caitlin surveyed the contents of the cart. "Let's do a quick recap. Two cans of cranberry sauce, ten pounds of potatoes, a dozen dinner rolls and the fixings for green bean casserole. Oh, and a bird large enough to feed at least a dozen people and still provide you with enough leftovers until Christmas."

"There's something missing."

"Pumpkin pie. Do you want to make them from scratch or buy them from the deli?"

While Devon mulled over the question, Caitlin added a bag of marshmallows in case he wanted to add sweet potato casserole to the menu.

When she'd gone out to dinner with her sisters, they'd applied the usual amount of pressure to get her to attend the family event otherwise known as Thanksgiving, but she still hadn't firmed up her own plans.

Evie had invited the entire family—Sam's relatives included—to their home, a refurbished lighthouse in Door County, but Caitlin's appointment calendar was booked solid right up until Thanksgiving Day. Meghan, whose schedule was more flexible, planned to extend her visit through the weekend but Caitlin didn't have that luxury. As much as she wanted to spend time with her family and see her father again, she wouldn't be able to make the long drive there and back in a single day. So she'd resigned herself to another Thanksgiving with Mr. Darcy.

Not that he wasn't good company.

"Marshmallows?" Devon peered into the cart.

"Haven't you ever had sweet potato casserole?"

"Not on purpose."

"It happens to be my specialty."

"Great. That can be your contribution."

What was she? A deli? "You want me to send over my sweet potato casserole?"

"No, I want you to *bring* your sweet potato casserole. When you come over for Thanksgiving."

Caitlin's breath hitched. Did he mean what it sounded like he meant? She was almost afraid to ask. "You're…inviting me over for Thanksgiving?"

"That's why you're helping me, isn't it?" Devon tossed

another bag of croutons, conveniently located in a bin next to the turkeys, into the cart. "We're in this together."

Together.

The word held a sweetness that tugged at her heart like a light in a window beckoned to a weary traveler.

"I thought you wanted a...personal shopper."

Devon stepped closer and the rest of the people in the crowded grocery store suddenly vanished. "I want *you*, Cait. To be there for Thanksgiving. And so do my children. Will you join us?"

The question hung in the air between them.

It's a simple dinner invitation, she reminded herself. Don't read anything else into it.

What are you afraid of, Caitlin?

Caitlin suddenly heard Evie's words as clearly as if she were standing in the aisle next to her. She'd managed to dodge her sisters' curiosity during dinner, but when they'd announced they were staying overnight at her condo, she knew they had her cornered.

She'd tried to convince her sisters there was nothing going on between her and Devon. Glaring had proven unsuccessful and changing the subject several times had only seemed to make their smiles grow wider.

And then Evie had spoken up—and the simple question had rattled Caitlin more than their good-natured teasing. She wasn't afraid of anything! She'd told them so. And they might have believed her if tears hadn't banked behind her eyes.

Caitlin had been horrified. She *never* got mushy and sentimental. At least she hadn't until she'd started spending time with the Walshes. They managed to mine emotions she didn't know existed.

All the boys had to do was shoot her one of their shy grins and she wanted to tousle their hair and then smooth it back into place. She wanted to encourage Jenny through the tweenage years and navigate her through the rough spots.

And Devon…she wanted to erase the tiny lines of concern that fanned out from his eyes. And she wanted to see him look at her the way he had when they'd washed dishes together. As if he trusted her. As if he…liked her.

The way he was looking at her now.

And *that's* what she was afraid of.

Because when he looked at her like that, she lost sight of everything else.

That's why she couldn't believe the words that came out of her mouth.

"I'd love to have Thanksgiving dinner with you."

Chapter Fifteen

"Why isn't Caitlin here yet?"

It was the third time in fifteen minutes that Jenny had asked the question. And now Devon was beginning to wonder the same thing.

"I'm sure she's just running a little late."

Jenny cast him a doubtful glance. "I don't think she likes late."

Devon couldn't argue with that. Caitlin, as Brady's stopwatch could attest, tended to be extremely punctual. She probably *didn't* like late.

She didn't like to blur professional boundaries, either, and yet she'd gone shopping with him and agreed to a cup of coffee at a mom-and-pop diner afterward. When Devon had dropped her off at her apartment, she'd promised she'd be over bright and early on Thanksgiving morning to help him get the turkey ready for the oven.

Would she really back out at the last minute?

And if she did, what was he supposed to tell Jenny and the boys?

"Why don't you go check on your brothers?" Devon suggested. "I'll keep an eye out for Caitlin."

The slam of a car door brought an instant smile to Jenny's face. "She's here."

Relief swept through Devon as his daughter raced down the hall and it wasn't only because he'd been saved from having to make up an excuse for Caitlin's absence.

Having Caitlin spend the day with them seemed…right.

She'd kept her promise. And now he was going to keep the one he'd made to himself that morning.

"I'm sorry I'm late." Caitlin handed Jenny a large canvas bag. "I had to make a few stops on the way over."

Devon could have sworn the color in her cheeks wasn't simply due to the chill in the air.

"What's in the bag?" Jenny asked curiously.

"A few traditions of my own." Caitlin gave the end of Jenny's ponytail a tug.

Sweet potato casserole. He supposed he could try it. Just to be polite.

The boys thundered down the stairs to say hello and danced around her, each one vying to give her the latest update on the ring, as she bent down to unlace her boots.

"Your dad is really cool," Brady said.

Josh nodded vigorously in agreement. "He wants us to visit him when the weather gets warmer. He's going to show us where they found *The Noble*."

"So I heard."

It was impossible to judge from the neutral tone how Caitlin felt about her father's invitation.

Devon, on the other hand, was already looking forward to a visit to Cooper's Landing.

He'd talked with Patrick McBride several times on the phone and had found the retired English teacher to have an easygoing personality coupled with a quick wit that reminded him of

Caitlin. But unlike his oldest daughter, Patrick had more of an open-door policy when it came to his life.

When the boys had pumped him for information about the shipwreck Patrick had discovered, he'd immediately invited them all for a visit, not only promising a tour of the museum where the gold coins from *The Noble* were on display but also a boat ride to the exact spot where salvage divers had located the remains of the ship.

As far as field trips went, Devon knew he couldn't top Patrick's generous offer.

"You'll be there, too, won't you, Caitlin?" Jenny took advantage of a momentary break in her brothers' chatter.

"It'll be fun," Brady said.

"Yeah—and Dad said you need to have some fun."

"He said that?" Caitlin's eyebrow lifted. At him.

Devon made a silent note to tell the twins that what was said at the dinner table, stayed at the dinner table.

Josh nodded. "That's why we made the piñata. We didn't paint it yet because Dad said you'd want to help."

"It looks like a turkey." Brady paused thoughtfully. "Kind of."

Caitlin's expression registered her confusion but it was obvious that she didn't want to spoil the boys' excitement.

"Didn't I mention that today was the day new Walsh family traditions were going to be started?" Devon reminded her.

"But a…piñata?"

The children giggled and Devon gave her a cheerful wink.

"Oh, that's only the beginning."

"This is it." Caitlin put the last fork back in the drawer and hung the damp dish cloth over a hook. She dropped into a chair at the kitchen table and closed her eyes. "I suggest you drop *exhaustion* from your list of new Walsh family traditions. Or else invest in a dishwasher."

Devon pulled out the chair opposite her and sat down. He didn't look a bit tired. "We did manage to squeeze quite a bit into the day, didn't we?"

Definitely an understatement.

"I'm not surprised the kids could barely make it up the stairs to get ready for bed." She slanted a meaningful glance at him. "I hope the paint comes off in the shower."

"It's washable. I checked the label. We definitely have to add the turkey piñata to our keeper list and make one again next year."

Next year.

After spending the day with Devon and his children, Caitlin was even more convinced they had to remain a family.

Lord, let them be together next year. Please.

Caitlin sent up the silent prayer even as the truth pierced her heart.

She wouldn't be with them next year.

But you want to be.

The realization stole the breath from her lungs.

During the course of the day, the footings underpinning Caitlin's plan to keep her distance had been slowly eroded by the sound of their laughter. The walls she'd carefully constructed around her heart weakened by the simplest things—a smile from Jenny. A tug on her sleeve from one of the boys when they wanted her attention.

She'd gone from feeling like a guest to feeling as if she belonged.

"I'm sorry if things got a little crazy around here," Devon went on, oblivious to the sound of Caitlin's defenses crumbling. "I've missed the past five holidays with them and I wanted to do…"

"Everything." Caitlin filled in the blank when Devon's voice cracked and he looked away, as if embarrassed by the show of emotion.

"Everything." He echoed the word.

Caitlin took a deep breath. Honesty called for honesty. "It wasn't a crazy day. It was…memorable. And I think they thought so, too."

"Memorable." Devon's eyes sparkled with sudden humor and Caitlin's heart, freed from its restraints, did a weird little hop-skip in response. "But still a bit beyond the realm of your typical Thanksgiving Day celebration?"

"A little." She amended the statement when he quirked an eyebrow. "Okay, a lot."

And it had started with the piñata.

Devon was right. Caitlin had never experienced a Thanksgiving quite like the one she'd just shared with Devon and his family.

After they'd put the turkey in the oven, the twins had led her to the parlor and excitedly pointed out the "other" turkey. The one they'd constructed out of papier-mâché. The one they wanted her to help them paint.

The bird's tail had ended up resembling a rainbow more than feathers and Caitlin had added her own personal touch—tipping its toenails with dabs of scarlet.

But it was Devon's fault she hadn't been the one to knock down the piñata. By the time he'd finished tying the blindfold around her eyes, she'd been so rattled by his casual touch that she almost took out a lamp instead of the intended target.

After several failed attempts by the boys, Jenny had been the one to finally break it open. They divided the spoils and then moved on to the next item on Devon's list of new Walsh Thanksgiving traditions.

Caitlin, who rarely gave in to her sisters' pleas to join in a game of Scrabble, played a staggering number of board games and completed a five-hundred-piece puzzle of the Statue of Liberty.

She'd tried to shoo everyone out of the kitchen while she tended to the last minute dinner preparations, but they ignored her hints. The result was a dinner that turned out well despite a few minor mishaps.

Right before Devon carved the turkey, his expression had grown serious. He asked them to bow their heads, join hands and take a few seconds to thank God for one of His blessings. Caitlin guessed it would be added to the list of Walsh family traditions.

She hadn't prayed in a group setting for a long time and she felt a little uncomfortable, but when it was her turn, the warm press of Devon's hand encouraged her. Out loud, Caitlin had thanked God for family and friendship.

In her heart, she'd been more specific. She'd thanked Him for Devon and his children.

The connection between her and Devon when they'd prayed together seemed more powerful than the laughter they'd shared over the course of the day or the camaraderie of working side by side in the kitchen.

Caitlin remembered padding down the stairs early in the morning and seeing her parents sitting on the couch together, hands clasped and their heads bent in prayer. She couldn't hear what they were saying but she'd felt safe and secure; knowing without a doubt some of those prayers were for her.

Maybe Devon didn't choose to wear designer labels, but his genuine faith added a depth to his personality that made other men seem shallow in comparison.

"We're ready for bed, Dad!" The chorus of voices traveled from the top of the stairs to the kitchen.

Devon heaved a sigh and rose to his feet. "Round two."

Caitlin knew his exaggerated response was an act. Devon didn't begrudge a single minute of time and energy spent on his children.

"Go ahead. I'll let myself out." Caitlin glanced at the clock and realized she'd missed "The Phone Call"—one of the McBride family traditions. Whenever they couldn't be together on a holiday, they had a standing rule to call each other at nine o'clock sharp.

They'd passed that deadline twenty minutes ago.

And now she'd have to explain why she hadn't answered the phone! Her sisters would never let her live this down. Especially since she'd been vague about her plans for the day to begin with.

"Stay for a few minutes." Devon's husky voice cut through Caitlin's rising panic. She was barely able to acknowledge her growing feelings for Devon; she certainly couldn't explain them to her family! "I have something for you. Something to say thank you for helping me make the day…memorable."

A thank-you. Caitlin wavered. She could accept a thank-you, couldn't she?

"Caitlin!" The voices had gotten closer. But this time the twins called out *her* name.

Devon grinned. "I think that's your cue."

"My cue?"

Josh and Brady appeared in matching flannel pajamas and raced to her side.

Brady tugged on her arm. "Come on. Your dad wants to say hi."

"My…" Caitlin choked. "Dad?"

"We're talking to him on the computer," Josh said.

Wonders never ceased, Caitlin thought. Patrick McBride, the man who couldn't find the power button on his computer a year and a half ago, was online. And now her entire family knew she'd spent the day with Devon and the kids.

Caitlin gave Devon a helpless look but he gestured toward the doorway, looking way too smug.

"After you."

Devon glanced over his shoulder and smiled when he saw Josh and Brady dive below their comforters. Seconds later, their miniature flashlights began to glow. The twins had created their own secret code using a series of long and short blinks and Devon guessed they were having another private conversation.

"Boys—don't stay up too late," Devon cautioned. "You need your sleep."

The lights under the covers flashed twice in response and Devon smiled.

Down the hall in Jenny's room, Caitlin's husky contralto blended with his daughter's in a soft, pleasing cadence.

Devon didn't mean to eavesdrop on their conversation, but when he heard Jenny say the word mom, he froze.

Somewhere along the line, he'd forgotten his concern about who Caitlin was and what she did for a living.

Because he'd started to think of her simply as Cait.

"Do you still miss your mom?" He heard Jenny ask.

"Every day."

"Do you still…cry?"

"No."

"Why not?"

"I guess I felt like it wouldn't honor her memory. She was such a strong woman. She faced things head-on and I guess I always wanted to be the same way."

Devon tensed. Was that the reason Caitlin kept such tight control over her emotions? It made sense in a strange sort of way.

"Dad says it's okay to cry—that feelings need an escape hatch."

"Your dad might be right." The words sounded so uncertain that Devon suppressed a smile.

"Caitlin? When are you coming back?"

The length of the silence that greeted his daughter's innocent question made Devon catch his breath.

"Your dad and I don't have a reason to…see each other anymore."

"Oh." Jenny sounded disappointed. "I was hoping you could teach me how to knit. I want to make a bag like yours."

"I don't…"

Have time.

Devon filled in the blank and his heart ached for his daughter. And for Caitlin. Spending the day with them obviously hadn't had as much of an impact on her as it had on him.

"I'll talk to your dad. Maybe we can go and pick out some yarn together. Would you like that?" Caitlin's tone was cautious, as if she were waiting for Jenny to say no.

"He'll say yes. Dad likes you," Jenny said blithely.

Devon wondered if Caitlin was blushing like he was.

"Good night, Caitlin."

"Good night…sweetheart."

Devon barely caught the last word because he backed away from the door before Caitlin caught him eavesdropping.

He had one more thing to cross off his list before they called it a day.

Chapter Sixteen

Caitlin turned off the light on the way out of Jenny's room, a little shaken by their conversation.

When she'd seen the tears in Jenny's eyes as she got ready for bed, Caitlin immediately guessed the reason. And she'd chided herself for not being more sensitive. As much as Jenny had enjoyed the day with Devon, this was the first holiday she'd spent without her mother.

Jenny's tentative question had confirmed it.

When Jenny had asked if she still cried, Caitlin had found that she couldn't lie to her. As a police officer, Laura McBride had faced dangerous and heartbreaking situations with confidence and grace. Caitlin had decided that she couldn't do any less.

After Laura died, she'd had to be there for her younger sisters and for her father. And even though Caitlin had felt as if something inside of her had broken beyond repair, she hadn't let it show. People had commented on the way her strength provided comfort to her family and how much she reminded them of her mother. Caitlin had absorbed their praise and made sure that none of her feelings leaked out to stain Laura's memory.

But Devon had told his daughter that feelings needed an escape hatch. Caitlin wasn't sure she agreed with that but she hadn't wanted to belittle his advice, either.

"Cait?"

Her heart leaped like a trained seal at the sound of Devon's voice.

"I'm getting my coat." And struggling to get her perspective back.

Devon had retreated to the kitchen to start a fire in the fireplace. When she hesitated in the doorway, he smiled.

"It's my room of choice now. Strong coffee within reach. No ductwork to transmit conversations."

Caitlin couldn't help but smile back. "My parents never did figure out how we knew about surprise birthday parties, family vacations or homework lectures in advance."

"I appreciated the heads-up." Devon sat back on his heels and watched the tiny flames curl around the kindling he'd stacked inside. "You can come in, you know. Unless you're afraid I'm going to ask you to clean the oven."

That wasn't what she was afraid of. She wasn't even afraid of Devon...she was afraid of *herself*. Her feelings. Caitlin felt like that kindling. Devon had somehow infiltrated her heart, fanning a spark that she was afraid would only grow stronger.

If she let it.

"I should be going. It's late." Caitlin pushed her hands into her pockets and her fingers closed around Brady's stopwatch. "Here, I almost forgot to give this to you."

The sudden tension in Devon's posture sent off warning bells in Caitlin's head.

"How did you get that? Brady hasn't let that stopwatch out of his sight since he moved in."

"He wanted to time how long it took to put the puzzle

together but I said that was the whole idea behind puzzles. No time limits. They take as long as they take. Like a lot of other things in life." She couldn't quite read Devon's expression. "He gave me the watch and never asked for it back."

Devon continued to stare at the watch as if he'd never seen it before.

"Is something wrong? Did I do something I shouldn't have?" She should have known eventually she'd mess up when it came to the children.

"Not at all. I—" Devon attempted a laugh. "You don't, ah, happen to know why Josh is afraid of the dark, do you?"

Caitlin thought about Josh, the sensitive, introspective one of Devon's dynamic duo. "If I had to guess, I'd say he was probably the brunt of a lot of practical jokes in the dorms at his private school."

Devon clapped a hand over his eyes. "Maybe you should write a parenting book. I'll even endorse it."

"Mmm." Caitlin chose to be tactful. "I'll keep that in mind."

"Be sure that you do. And on that note, I promised to give you a thank-you for coming over today." Devon retrieved some books from the table. "You mentioned you wanted the Ransom series for your niece."

Caitlin shuffled through the stack of paperback novels in astonishment. "There's four of them…you bought the fourth one already? Where did you find it?"

He lifted one shoulder in a modest shrug. "I have some connections."

"They're signed by the author?" Caitlin brushed her thumb across the gold sticker in the bottom corner before flipping open the cover on one of the books.

Sure enough, the name D. Birch was scrawled unevenly across the page.

"How did you get these autographed? Birch signs under a

pseudonym, doesn't he? Even the publisher's Web site is cagey about who he really is."

That appealing twitch played at the corner of Devon's lips. "No kidding."

"Haven't you looked him up on the Internet? He's as much of a mystery as his…mysteries. There are no pictures of him. No biography. He doesn't do book signings or tours. He's a recluse. A modern-day hermit. He's…" The pieces suddenly fell into place and Caitlin stared at him in disbelief. "You. You're *him*. Aren't you?"

Devon shrugged. "I can neither confirm nor deny that I'm D. Birch."

He didn't have to deny it. If Caitlin had been paying closer attention to detail—and she prided herself on that quality—she would have guessed it sooner.

Devon had fictionalized his own story.

A father separated from his children. A desperate struggle to be reunited in spite of the overwhelming odds against them. Each book in the series featured a different adventure, filled with unexpected twists and turns, that brought them closer to being together.

Another thought struck her. The series was extremely successful. Which meant the *author* was extremely successful. According to the jacket, the third book had hit the young adult bestseller list the year before.

"You *lied* to me! You said you were a poet."

Devon looked offended. "I never lied to you—I do happen to write poetry. It's just not very good. And it's not how I make my living."

Caitlin's fingers tightened around the books. "Why all the secrecy?"

Devon's gaze shifted to the fireplace again. "I want to write. I don't want publicity."

"But you could use it to your advantage."

He didn't move, but she felt a chasm open up between them. "No."

"You plan to tell the judge who are you, don't you? When it comes time for the custody hearing?"

Devon's jaw tightened, answering her question, and Caitlin sighed in frustration. "I appreciate your disguise, Mr. Walsh, but if the judge knows you're a successful author, it might tip the favor in your balance. Isn't Vickie under the impression that you don't have a steady job?"

"So I should use my celebrity stature and walk into the courtroom as D. Birch because Devon Walsh isn't good enough." A bitter edge scored the words.

"Devon Walsh is a great father. He's also a man who's trying to prove something. But in my opinion, the only thing he's proving is that he's stubborn." Caitlin saw Devon's eyes darken to onyx and knew she'd touched a nerve.

"You don't understand."

Caitlin didn't back down. "Enlighten me."

To her amazement, the tension in Devon's shoulders eased and he gave her a rueful smile. "I have reasons for wanting to keep my private life private."

"I'm sure you do," Caitlin said softly. "But you also have three very good reasons to swallow your pride and let people know who you are. All of them."

His eyebrow rose. "As much as writers are warned to avoid clichés, isn't this the pot calling the kettle black?"

Touché, Caitlin thought. And she'd thought they didn't have anything in common! "I think it's time to say goodnight now."

"You're running away?"

Caitlin wished she hadn't kicked her shoes off earlier. It gave him a distinct advantage.

"I never run away." Her chin rose. "I just…plan a new direction."

Devon's low burst of laughter plowed a furrow right through her heart. "Do you know what I think? I think that before you go, there's one more tradition I'd like to add."

"I'm pretty sure you already passed the allowed quota for Thanksgiving Day trad—"

Devon drew her into his arms, his kiss capturing the rest of the word.

Devon hadn't planned to kiss her.

She was just so…*Cait.* Maddening. Adorable. Challenging him one minute, making him laugh the next.

Her hands settled on his waist and the logical side of Devon's brain—which was rapidly diminishing in capacity—waited for her to push him away. To let him know he'd crossed a line.

She didn't. For one heart-stopping moment, she tentatively leaned into the embrace. And she fit into his arms as if she'd been made for them.

Devon wanted to keep her there.

Instead, he broke the connection first and took an uneven step away from her.

"Caitlin, I—" Devon tried to come up with something. An excuse. An apology. Anything that would explain why he'd kissed her. His brain refused to cooperate. That simple kiss had wielded the force of a nuclear explosion and he was still suffering from the fallout.

"I should go." The undisguised panic in her eyes caught his attention.

Instinctively, Devon reached out to her but she stepped away.

"I didn't…plan that." It was the best he could do. He wasn't going to apologize for something that he didn't regret.

"Thank you for inviting me over today." Caitlin's voice

sounded stilted. Polite. As if she hadn't been in the circle of his arms moments before. "You shouldn't need anything else from IMAGEine, but if you do, don't hesitate to call Sabrina."

You shouldn't need anything else from IMAGEine.

It was funny, Devon thought, *how much she conveyed in that formal little farewell speech.* As if she was reminding him that she and IMAGEine weren't separate. Didn't she understand that she was a business *owner,* not a business?

What about your promise to Jenny, Devon wanted to say as she walked away. But he couldn't; not without letting her know he'd eavesdropped on her conversation with his daughter.

"I'll let myself out."

Out of his house. Out of their lives.

It hadn't been that long ago that Devon couldn't imagine Caitlin being part of his life. Now he was having a difficult time imagining it without her.

Devon closed his eyes.

I messed up, Lord. Now what?

The answer came swiftly. And it made Devon smile.

"He changed the rules again."

Mr. Darcy, amazingly capable of multitasking, lifted one crooked ear to listen to her lament while grooming his whiskers.

All day long Caitlin had been fighting her attraction for Devon, never dreaming that he might share her feelings.

Did she want him to? Up to this point, she'd kept the borders around her life closed. She hadn't dated since college, afraid that opening the door to a relationship would take her mind off her goals.

She'd been right.

Spending the day with Devon and his children had her looking forward to the next one. Imagining another Thanksgiving piñata. Another kiss…

Caitlin closed her eyes.

She'd become adept at sticking to a course she'd set while still in her early twenties.

I'm doing the right thing, aren't I, God?

For the first time Caitlin posed it as a question instead of a statement. And for the first time, she waited for an answer.

Chapter Seventeen

"When you wake up in the middle of the night and feel like you should pray for someone, what do you do?"

"Caitlin?" Meghan sounded groggy. "What time is it?"

"Seven-thirty. Now answer the question."

Ever since she'd gotten up, Caitlin had ignored the overwhelming nudge to call Devon and make sure everything was all right. She lined up her shoes in the closet, folded a load of laundry and tried to knit. But no matter how busy she kept her hands, her thoughts had refused to cooperate.

She finally broke down and called her sister.

Meghan yawned. "I pray for them, of course."

"But how do you know it wasn't just a feeling? Or too much garlic in the pasta?"

"If God puts someone on your heart, there's a reason."

Meghan's approach to faith always seemed so simple. *But then again,* Caitlin thought, *maybe she was the one who complicated it.*

"Thanks, Megs."

"Anytime. Good night."

Caitlin didn't correct her. As soon as she hung up the phone, she dialed Devon's number before she lost her nerve.

"Hello."

Caitlin's fingers tightened around the phone at the curt greeting. "It's…Cait."

"Cait." Warmth seeped into Devon's tone and found a path straight to Caitlin's heart. They hadn't seen each other for over a week but was it possible he'd missed the sound of her voice as much as she'd missed his? "How are you?"

"Why don't you answer that question first. Is everything all right with you?"

"Define all right. The boys both came down with colds that turned into ear infections, so I'm taking them to the pediatrician this afternoon. My deadline for the proposal on book five is next Friday." He paused. "I'm whining, aren't I? I doubt you called to listen to me go on and on."

He had no idea, Caitlin thought, *that that was exactly the reason she'd called.*

"It sounds like you're entitled." Caitlin strived to match the lightness of his tone.

"So." Devon cleared his throat. "What's going on with you?"

Translation: Why was she calling? And what was she supposed to say? That she woke up from a sound sleep at two o'clock in the morning, struck by an overwhelming urge to pray for him?

"I called to…." She lost her nerve, still in awe of the fact that once she'd opened up the communication lines to God, He'd begun to show her that it wasn't a one-way street. "Is there, ah, anything I can do to help?"

Dead silence.

Caitlin frowned. "Devon? Are you still there?"

"Sorry. Yeah, I'm still here."

She heard a stifled yawn on the other end of the line and came to a decision. "I have some shopping to do for a client this afternoon at the Mall of America. Do you think Jenny would like to tag along with me while you take the boys to the doctor?"

"I'm sure she'd love that." Devon sounded shocked by the offer.

So was Caitlin. But she missed Jenny and the boys, too. And Devon sounded tired...

"Great. We'll do lunch, too. I'll pick her up in half an hour."

"I'll make sure she's ready." And Cait?" Devon hesitated. "Thanks."

Caitlin hung up the phone.

"You're welcome," she said softly.

"You look terrible."

Devon grinned. "Is that an official evaluation from my certified image consultant or sympathy from a friend?"

Caitlin didn't answer but the color blooming in her cheeks proved she wasn't immune to the sparks between them. Sparks he'd unwittingly ignited when he'd kissed her goodbye.

Devon knew he'd overstepped his bounds so he had to be the one to back off and create some space between them. And if Devon were completely honest with himself, he'd needed some time to regain his balance, too.

When almost a week had gone by without a word from Caitlin, he could only assume that that impulsive kiss had severed the tenuous bond between them.

Her phone call that morning—and her offer to help—had given Devon hope that he hadn't totally blown it. And it wasn't until after he'd hung up the phone that Devon realized how much Caitlin had changed him. Not only on the outside, but on the inside. Where it counted the most.

After Ashleigh walked out on him and took their kids away, Devon had felt as if his life had become a wasteland. Over time, his faith had slowly reshaped the landscape but he hadn't expected to fall in love again. Or trust again.

But that's exactly what was happening. Because after Devon had hung up the phone, it occurred to him that he'd trusted Caitlin to take his daughter out for the day. Alone.

"Where are the boys?" Caitlin asked.

"In the kitchen getting a glass of juice. Neither one of them have felt like eating much the past few days." Devon paused. "Did you want to say hello?"

Caitlin looked uncertain. "I brought a little something to cheer them up. But you can give it to them."

Devon turned away so she wouldn't see him smile. Caitlin might try to keep her distance, but didn't she know that her actions revealed her heart?

"No, go ahead. Jenny's still upstairs getting ready."

"All right."

He followed her into the kitchen where the boys were slumped against the table, matching expressions of misery on their faces.

They both brightened visibly when they saw Caitlin. Devon wondered briefly if he'd looked the same way.

"Hey, guys. Your dad said you aren't feeling very well." Without hesitation, Caitlin positioned herself between the boys, who melted against her like chocolate in the sun.

"Where've you been?" Brady asked, as if Caitlin's continued presence had been something he'd expected to occur on a regular basis.

Devon decided to rescue her from the awkward silence. "Caitlin has been busy at work, guys."

Caitlin didn't deny it as she pulled two packages out of her knitted bag and handed one to each of the boys.

"Presents? Cool!" Without ceremony, they ripped off the colorful paper she'd used to wrap them.

Devon inched closer, curious to see what she'd brought.

"Spy stuff!"

Before Caitlin could react, Devon's sons had attached them-selves to her, winding their arms around her in a damp, feverish hug.

"Hey, guys. Say thank you, don't strangle the poor woman."

"Thanks, Caitlin." Josh and Brady obediently released Caitlin and began to attack the boxes.

Caitlin's smile seemed almost…shy as she watched them comparing the contents.

"Spy stuff?" Devon murmured. "I thought you were on Dr. Chamberlain's side."

"Not anymore," Caitlin whispered back. "I think that the sooner the Ransom boys are reunited with their father, the better."

Devon didn't know what to say. But he knew what he wanted to do. He wanted to kiss….

"I'm ready, Caitlin!" Jenny sang from the doorway.

Devon didn't miss the spark of happiness in his daughter's eyes. Even though Jenny hadn't come right out and asked when Caitlin was coming back, she had mentioned that Caitlin planned to teach her to knit. Devon hadn't had the heart to contradict her. To tell her that thanks to good old dad's impulsive decision to "add another tradition" they might never see Caitlin again.

He was really glad Caitlin had spared him that particular conversation.

"I'll have her back by supper," Caitlin said.

Devon took another risk. "Will you stay? I'll make spaghetti."

For a split second, Caitlin looked as if she were about to turn him down. "I'd like that."

"I wasn't expecting to see you today. Is this business or pleasure?" Dawn Gallagher slid into an empty chair across the table from Caitlin, her curious gaze lighting briefly on Jenny.

Caitlin silently groaned. Thousands of pre-Christmas shoppers and they had to run into Dawn. What were the chances?

Now she wished she and Jenny had chosen a more secluded table at one of the sit-down restaurants rather than one in the crowded café court.

Caitlin forced a smile. "Both. One of my clients needed accessory support."

"Is she talking about you?" Dawn shifted her gaze back to Jenny and her eyes widened.

Jenny ducked her head. "N-no."

Dawn continued to stare intently at the girl. "You look familiar. Have I seen you somewhere before?"

"Dawn, this is Jenny Walsh." Caitlin reluctantly made the introduction, knowing it was too much to hope the style editor wouldn't recognize her name. "Jenny, this is my friend, Dawn Gallagher."

"Hi." Jenny managed a shy smile.

"Walsh." Dawn's eyes narrowed. "You're the girl who entered your dad in the makeover contest?"

Jenny nodded and shifted uncomfortably in the chair. Caitlin suddenly understood Devon's protective instincts toward his children.

"Well, well." Dawn flicked a glance at Caitlin and the temperature in the air around them dropped several degrees. "I didn't realize you'd taken her on as a client."

Caitlin could see the path her thoughts were going down and intercepted her before she reached the wrong conclusion. That Caitlin had been holding out on her. "Jenny isn't a client. She's a friend. We're having a girls' afternoon out."

"How…sweet." Dawn dumped the packages on the chair next to the one she'd already claimed. "I'm exhausted. You don't mind sharing your table, do you?"

"We're almost finished but have a seat." Caitlin had suddenly lost her appetite.

The suspicion in Dawn's eyes said she didn't believe

Caitlin's explanation. In Dawn's mind, if Caitlin spent time with someone, it somehow had to benefit her career.

The reality left a bitter taste in Caitlin's mouth. Because before she'd met Devon, it would have been true.

"How is your dad, by the way?" Dawn asked, once again turning her attention to Jenny.

"He's good."

"Keeping busy, I suppose. What did you say that he does for a living, Caitlin?"

She hadn't.

"He's self-employed." Caitlin pushed the carton containing the remains of a double order of sesame chicken onto the tray. "Are you finished, Jenny? We still have a few more stops to make."

"Sounds like you're in a rush." The edge in Dawn's voice once again questioned their outing. "Did you find anything special, Jenny? You're with a professional, you know. You should take advantage of her."

Caitlin's stomach flipped. The gleam in the other woman's eyes made her uneasy.

Was Dawn still trying to manipulate a way to use Devon? Caitlin wouldn't put it past her. She'd heard a rumor that Dawn's senior editor at *Twin City Trends* was still unhappy with the magazine's dropping sales.

"We haven't had much time to shop," Caitlin intervened. "Jenny wanted a new haircut and Valeria insisted on giving her her famous skincare lecture."

"No makeup lesson?" Dawn barely acknowledged Caitlin as she continued to study Jenny, who'd followed Caitlin's lead and started to collect her things.

"Jenny doesn't need makeup yet. There's plenty of time for that." Caitlin tried to draw Dawn's attention away from Jenny again, like a mother duck pretending to have a broken wing to give her babies an opportunity to take cover.

Dawn's nostrils flared in irritation, a direct contrast to the smile she directed at Jenny.

"How old are you? Fourteen? Fifteen?"

"Almost thirteen." Jenny beamed at what any girl her age would perceive as a compliment but Caitlin winced. It hadn't been her imagination that the shorter, trendy haircut had made Jenny look older.

She wondered what Devon's reaction would be. She'd taken his little girl away and brought back a young woman!

"Practically a teenager." Dawn gave Jenny a conspiratorial wink. "Why don't I take a picture of you both to officially document your girls' day out?"

Before Caitlin could respond, Dawn slipped a digital camera out of her purse and aimed it at them. Jenny wilted against Caitlin's side as the flash went off. Caitlin wrapped her arm around Jenny's shoulders and gave her a reassuring squeeze.

"Take a look." Dawn held out the camera. "Jenny is very photogenic. But that's not really a surprise, is it?"

"No." *Not when Devon had passed on those beautifully sculpted cheekbones,* Caitlin thought, barely glancing at the image of her and Jenny framed in the tiny screen. "Take care, Dawn. It was…" Nice to see you again? Caitlin decided she couldn't tell a lie. "Have a good weekend."

Dawn smiled at Jenny. "Guaranteed."

Devon administered two doses of antibiotics, tucked the boys back into bed with a popular DVD and tried to scrape up some creativity as he flipped open his laptop.

Thanks to Caitlin, he'd become all too familiar with a troublesome little condition known as writer's block. Every time he started typing, she popped up in his thoughts.

Devon had finally retaliated by putting her in the story.

Of course he had to stay true to the all-characters-are-a-product-of-the-author's-imagination disclaimer in the front of the book but no one could say that the combination of dark hair and blue eyes wasn't common. Or that it wasn't a coincidence the mysterious woman introduced in chapter three happened to possess the skills to change a person's identity with a cache of theater makeup and wigs....

"We're home." Jenny's voice echoed in the stairwell.

We're home.

Devon could get used to hearing that.

He took the stairs two at a time and followed the sound of their voices to the kitchen, where a double recipe of spaghetti sauce simmered on the back of the stove. Barring any unforeseen disasters—and those happened to occur on a regular basis—they'd eat supper together and then he planned to get Caitlin alone.

They needed to talk.

"You two were gone a long time. I hope that doesn't mean you bought out the whole mall—" Devon's voice died in his throat at the sight of his daughter. At least, he thought it was his daughter. The girl standing next to Caitlin looked a lot different from the girl who'd left the house a few hours before.

"Do you like it?" Jenny grinned and performed a graceful pirouette. "Caitlin's friend cut it. We bought some new clothes, too."

Because first impressions last?

Devon fought the urge to say the words out loud. He glanced at Caitlin but could barely see her through the red haze that suddenly clouded his vision.

"An early Christmas gift." Caitlin smiled down at Jenny.

"I got a skin-care lesson, too," Jenny continued. "The lady said I don't need to worry about makeup right now but Caitlin thinks lip gloss is okay when you're my age."

"Is that what Caitlin thinks?" Devon flicked a look at Caitlin and saw her frown.

"I'm going to show Josh and Brady." Jenny fluffed up the ends of her hair with her fingers and tossed her head in a gesture so familiar that it swept Devon back in time. He hadn't realized how much Jenny resembled Ashleigh. Until now.

How could he have been so blind? Jenny's striking resemblance to her mother gave her the potential to follow in Ashleigh's footsteps.

Fear clamped around Devon's heart. Maybe that had been Vickie's motive all along. She'd lost the opportunity to manage Ashleigh's career but she could still hobnob with the rich and famous if she groomed Jenny to take her sister's place.

And one afternoon with Caitlin could have set his daughter's foot on that path. He'd never seen Jenny so animated before. And he'd certainly never seen her spin circles in the kitchen or pause to admire her reflection in the toaster!

Jenny darted past him and Devon waited until he heard her footsteps fade before he faced Caitlin.

"What," he said softly, "do you think you're doing?"

Chapter Eighteen

Caitlin tensed at the rumble of anger in Devon's voice but stood her ground. "I'm not sure what you mean," she said cautiously. "You knew we planned a girls' day out."

"I didn't know that meant turning my twelve-year-old daughter into a miniature...pop star."

Caitlin gaped at him. There was nothing inappropriate about the outfit they'd bought and certainly nothing edgy about Jenny's shorter hairstyle. "Jenny wanted to surprise you—she said she was tired of how long it takes to wash and dry her hair."

Devon's expression didn't change. "And of course you encouraged her."

"I did." Caitlin couldn't deny it. She wouldn't have spoiled Jenny's obvious delight for the world. "I thought you wanted Jenny to gain some confidence. To come out of her shell."

"That doesn't mean I want her to become obsessed with her looks." Devon's fists clenched at his sides. "She's a little girl. Growing up is a process...it comes naturally. She doesn't need someone pushing her into it."

By someone, he meant her. Caitlin refused to let him see how much that statement hurt.

"Jenny isn't going to become obsessed with her looks, Devon, but it is okay for her to *like* them. To be comfortable in her own skin. I've got clients in their forties and fifties still wrestling with that and it trickles into other areas of their lives. The sooner Jenny learns to accept the way God made her and to work with what she has, the stronger she'll be. The women who *don't* operate out of that framework are the ones who become obsessed."

Devon's eyes darkened. She wasn't getting through to him. *Where is this coming from, Lord?*

Caitlin sent up a silent plea for understanding. A harmless day of shopping and a trip to the salon shouldn't have detonated a reaction like this.

He pivoted away from her. "I have to check on the boys."

"Devon—"

"Send me the bill for your time and I'll write you a check."

Caitlin sucked in a breath as the verbal arrow made a direct hit on her unprotected heart.

Devon strode out of the room without a backward glance.

The snick of the front door closing told Devon that she'd left but Caitlin's departure didn't do anything for his peace of mind. If anything, he felt worse.

"Dad?" Jenny's voice called out to him and Devon put on his game face before he went into her room.

"Hey, kiddo. What's up?"

"Is Caitlin still here?" Jenny sat cross-legged on her bed, a jaunty newsboy cap perched on her head.

"No." Devon forced the word out. "She had to leave."

"But I thought she—"

"Where did you get the hat?" Devon was always reminding the children it wasn't polite to interrupt but he decided to make an exception.

"Caitlin bought it for me." Jenny's smile lit up the room. "We tried on a bazillion but this is the one I liked the best. She bought one, too. She said a hat is the best cure for a bad day."

"Don't you mean a bad hair day?"

"Nope—just a bad day." Jenny sounded certain that's what Caitlin had said.

Devon sat down on the edge of the bed. "I thought you didn't like to shop."

"I don't. But it was fun to go with Caitlin."

"That's because shopping is part of her job, sweetie," Devon pointed out quietly. "It's what she gets paid to do and she's good at it."

"No, it's not." Jenny's expression was earnest. "We're friends. She even told Ms. Gallagher that. We're going to the art museum and out for Mexican next time, because it's my turn to pick."

"But what about your hair?" Devon clung stubbornly to his initial theory, afraid of what it would mean if he let in the doubts beginning to hammer against his thick skull.

The light in her eyes dimmed. "Don't you like it?"

"I love it." He realized it was the truth, now that the initial shock was wearing off. "But you didn't have to let Caitlin talk you into something so drastic, honey."

"She didn't talk me into it. I didn't like it long but Mom..." Jenny bit her lip.

Devon's heart bottomed out and he wasn't sure how much stress it could take in a day. But this was about Jenny, not him. "What about Mom?"

Jenny twisted the fringe on one of her pillows and refused to look at him. Devon had a hunch that loyalty to her mother's memory kept her silent. But he'd recently learned that silence only added to the weight of a burden.

"Mom didn't want you to get your hair cut," he guessed. "Why not?"

"She said it would make my face look...chubby. But Caitlin

said we women think about hair way too much and if I liked short hair, I should get it cut." The words came out in a rush and the tears followed. "Mom never liked the way I looked. She said she wasn't going to show me off until I got older. But she meant *prettier*. Like her. I know she did. And I didn't have time to *get* prettier before she…before she…"

Devon pulled his daughter into his arms and the truth began to work its way through the dense layers of his stubborn pride.

He was a first-class idiot.

Because the change he'd witnessed in his daughter—the glimmer of newfound confidence and the sparkle in her eyes—wasn't because of a new hairstyle or clothes. It didn't even have anything to with *shopping* with Caitlin.

It had everything to do with *being* with Caitlin.

Caitlin's cell phone rang just as she stumbled through the door of her apartment.

Was it Devon? Launching a second attack?

She decided to let the answering machine absorb the impact first.

"If you're there, Caitlin, pick up."

Caitlin's ragged sigh of relief woke Mr. Darcy up from his nap. She didn't want to talk to anyone but something in Dawn's tone gave her pause. Especially taking into consideration the style editor's strange behavior at the mall that afternoon.

"Hi, Dawn."

"Hi, yourself. I can't believe you've been holding out on me. I thought we were a team."

"Holding out…what are you talking about?" Caitlin pressed her fingers to her temple to ward off the headache she could feel coming on.

"Jenny Walsh, that's what I'm talking about."

"I told you. We're friends."

"Sure you are. I guess it pays to have *friends* in high places, doesn't it?" Dawn's voice dripped with sarcasm. "Maybe that's why you kept such a juicy little tidbit of information to yourself. So you could benefit from it."

Caitlin's heart stalled. Had Dawn somehow found out that Devon was the author of the Ransom mysteries?

"I'm not keeping anything to myself. It's not my fault Devon wasn't interested in participating in the makeover contest."

"*Devon* wasn't interested," Dawn repeated, emphasizing her use of his first name. "So what's he doing with you? Getting some tips before he goes public?"

She had found out.

"Just leave it alone, Dawn. It's none of your business."

"It's news," Dawn retorted. "And you've been keeping it to yourself long enough. I thought she looked familiar but I found an old picture in the magazine's archives a little while ago that confirmed it."

Caitlin slumped into the chair. "Who looks familiar? Who are you talking about?"

"You're too smart to play dumb. You know as well as I do that Jenny is a younger version of Ashleigh Heath—"

"Ashleigh Heath the *model?*" Caitlin choked on a laugh. Maybe Dawn didn't know about Devon after all. "You think I'm trying to cash in on Jenny's resemblance to a model?"

"No, on Jenny's resemblance to her mother."

When the doorbell rang a few hours later, Devon prayed that it was Caitlin—responding in person to the messages he'd left on her answering machine and voice mail.

"Devon Walsh?"

"Yes." Devon's hackles instantly rose at the sight of the young man with an expensive camera slung over his shoulder.

"I'm a reporter from *Twin City*—"

"No comment."

"I know you were married to the late Ashleigh Heath," he said quickly as the door began to close. "If I could get a brief statement...."

"I said no comment."

"The public has a right to know how her children are doing since the plane crash."

Unbelievable. "And we have a right to our privacy. Good night."

Devon shut the door and leaned against it. He didn't want to believe Caitlin had used an afternoon alone with his daughter for her own gain but Jenny had mentioned they'd had lunch with Dawn Gallagher. It had only taken a few seconds to match the name to the style editor working with Caitlin on the makeover feature.

And to think he'd been trying to get in touch with Caitlin to apologize....

Devon watched out the window until the darkness swallowed the reflection of the headlights and then he slowly mounted the stairs. He'd already checked on the kids once but felt the need to repeat the routine one more time.

The boys moved under the blankets in a restless sleep and Devon anticipated one more long night before the antibiotics began to work. He left the door open so he could hear them call out if they needed him and moved to Jenny's room.

She'd fallen asleep with the lamp on, curled up like a kitten with one arm thrown over her eyes and the other tucked underneath her head.

Devon padded over to the bed to turn out the light and saw the photographs on the nightstand. Caitlin and Jenny. They'd obviously ducked into one of those photo booths at the mall.

He picked up one of the strips and studied it. This one had been taken before Jenny got her hair cut and she looked self-conscious, as if posing for a candid shot ranked right up there with an oral book report. Caitlin had joined her for the rest of the shots and even though Jenny's smile looked a little less stiff, she hadn't looked directly into the camera lens.

Devon set that one carefully back in place and turned his attention to the next one. His breath caught in his throat. In the second strip, Caitlin and Jenny mugged for the camera in the hats they'd bought. The photos were taken after Jenny's haircut and facial but there was no way they could be mistaken for glamour shots. Because Caitlin McBride, professional image consultant, had her eyes crossed and her tongue sticking out. Jenny looked straight at the camera lens, an exaggerated pout on her face.

In the last image, they grinned at the camera, cheek to cheek. The sparkle in Jenny's eyes ignited a tremor that coursed through Devon and shook the photo strip in his hand.

Had it been Caitlin's plan all along to get him to let his guard down so that she could get close to his family? She prided herself on being a planner but he didn't want to believe she'd planned this.

I trusted her, Lord.

Chapter Nineteen

"I brought you some hot chocolate."

"Thanks, Dad." Patrick McBride's voice warmed Caitlin more than the steam rising from the mug her father offered. "It's a little chilly out there tonight."

"Um…yes." Patrick cleared his throat. "Don't take this the wrong way, sweetheart, but is everything all right?"

Everything, Caitlin thought, *is falling apart.* But she'd perfected the technique of hiding her emotions. She arched a brow. "Can't a girl pop in to visit her dad?"

"Most girls don't pop in at midnight," Patrick pointed out gently.

Caitlin felt a stab of guilt. And not only in response to her father's blurry-eyed confusion when he'd found her standing at the front door in the middle of the night. But because Caitlin Rae McBride—the one who always tackled problems head-on—had done something totally unscheduled and unpredictable.

She'd run away from home.

She'd packed a suitcase and stuffed a grumpy Mr. Darcy into his deluxe cat carrier, her destination uncertain. Until it began to dawn on her that the route she was traveling was a familiar one. One that would take her right to Cooper's Landing. To her father.

"I have a few days off." Something she'd have to let Sabrina know before Monday morning.

Patrick opened the doors on the fireplace and stirred the coals back to life with an iron poker. Silence stretched between them and Caitlin realized her father was at a loss. As if he didn't know how to respond to her impulsive visit.

She didn't blame him. She wasn't sure how to respond to it, either. *Impulsive* wasn't a word in her vocabulary.

"I put an extra blanket on the bed in the guest room."

"Thanks." Caitlin's voice sounded hollow. "You can go back to bed, Dad. I forgot that you aren't a night owl like me."

She'd forgotten a lot of things. Her sisters had remained close to their father, but she'd been so busy building her reputation as an image consultant that she hadn't devoted as much time to family relationships as she should have. If her sisters hadn't continually barged into her life, she probably would have let those relationships slide, too.

The truth scraped against Caitlin's already tender soul.

"I'll have the coffee on in the morning. Strong, just the way you like it." Patrick bent down and kissed her on top of the head as if she were a child again, rather than a successful, thirty-two-year-old businesswoman.

Tears banked in the back of Caitlin's eyes as her father padded out of the room. Mr. Darcy flicked a glance at her before bounding after him.

Caitlin took a deep breath. The numbness encasing her emotions during the long drive to Cooper's Landing had started to wear off, weakening her resolve against the thoughts she'd been trying to hold at bay. She gave up and let them in.

A custody battle. Boarding school in Europe. Devon's reclusive tendencies. His decision to teach his children at home while they settled in to being a family again.

Caitlin had thought they were signs pointing to a man who wanted to protect his anonymity. Instead, he'd been trying to protect Jenny and the boys. He'd even made tremendous sacrifices when it came to his own career in an effort to stay out of the spotlight. To create a normal home—one that his children could come back to.

Scrolling through the photos on her laptop—no doubt the same ones Dawn had looked through after she'd seen Jenny at the mall—Caitlin couldn't believe she hadn't seen the marked resemblance between Jenny and Ashleigh Heath before.

But there it was. A reporter had somehow gotten close enough to the mourners at Ashleigh's private funeral service to photograph Jenny and her brothers standing in the protective circle of Devon's arms.

On some subconscious level, Jenny's unusual copper-colored eyes had looked familiar but Caitlin hadn't made the connection. Then again, it wasn't surprising, considering she didn't pay much attention to the modeling world. Her job focused on helping women accept the woman in the mirror—not encouraging them to compare themselves to what culture held up as an ideal.

Caitlin forced herself to continue the search through Devon's past. Every photo, every article, came together like the pieces of a puzzle…and whittled off chunks of her heart in the process.

The earliest articles centered on Ashleigh—a young wife and mother—being discovered by a talent scout in the diner where she'd worked. The photos accompanying her rising career reflected the woman's luminous beauty and engaging girl-next-door smile. But after Ashleigh had become the spokeswoman for Kismet Cosmetics, her natural beauty had become more polished. The smile more worldly.

Occasionally a reporter mentioned Devon, almost as an afterthought, but there weren't many photos of him. Several had been taken at charity functions early in Ashleigh's career and he'd looked uncomfortable with all the attention.

There'd been a change in him, too. In his early twenties, Devon had possessed clean-cut, almost boyish, good looks. At that point, pain hadn't chiseled his jaw into a sharp line or stripped the hope from his eyes.

The last photo Caitlin found of Devon was the one a photographer had taken of him emerging from the courthouse after the custody hearing; his devastated expression didn't need a headline. The article leaned heavily on Ashleigh's side, citing her desire "to give her children all the opportunities she never had."

But what about the opportunities you denied them, Caitlin wanted to shout. To get to know their father…and each other.

Ashleigh might have had the best of intentions but she hadn't provided the things that Devon had. An active role in their lives. Laughter. Acceptance. *Love.*

What am I supposed to do now, Lord? Devon isn't going to believe I didn't have anything to do with bringing the reporters to his door.

Caitlin shut down the program and closed her eyes. That's what hurt the most. That Devon thought her capable of doing something that she knew would hurt them.

Dawn would take the story to her editor on Monday morning and the reporters would circle the Walshes' house like vultures to get a glimpse of Jenny—the girl she'd unwittingly helped transform into a younger version of her mother.

Caitlin could only pray that it wouldn't take long for the fickle media to focus their attention on someone else. Once they got what they wanted, they moved on, tracking the next big story.

She sat up straight, struck by a sudden thought that had her reaching for the phone.

A sleepy voice answered on the fifth ring. "'Lo?"

"Rob, this is Caitlin McBride—"

"What time is it?"

"Almost one."

An audible groan followed her announcement. "In the *morning*? Don't you ever sleep?"

"Only when absolutely necessary. But this is important. I need your help."

"Wait a second." The voice on the other end of the line sounded more alert. "I must be dreaming. Did you just say you needed…help?"

Caitlin rolled her eyes. "That's what I said."

"No kidding. With what?"

She told him.

Caitlin woke up to the sound of purring. Mr. Darcy had settled inches away from her face, happily kneading the pillow next to hers.

She heard a soft tap on the door.

"Caitlin? Are you awake?"

Time to face the music, Caitlin thought. And her father.

Patrick had been thrown off guard when she'd knocked on the door, but as an early riser, he had had time to regroup. And call her sisters to see if they could shed any light on her nocturnal visit!

"I thought you might like some breakfast while it's still hot."

Caitlin wanted to hide underneath the pile of quilts on the bed. Which was more disturbing than discovering Mr. Darcy could purr.

"Sure," she heard herself say. "I'll be up in a few minutes."

After Caitlin finished getting dressed, the distinct aroma of pancakes and maple syrup guided her to the kitchen. Another favorite of hers that her father had filed away in his memory.

The smile of genuine delight on Patrick's face snuffed out any lingering guilt she'd had over her arrival. He poured another cup of coffee and pushed a Blue Willow plate, stacked high with buttermilk pancakes, toward her.

Caitlin forced a smile and slumped into the chair opposite her father, feeling the effects of the sleepless night she'd endured. Even after talking with Rob, she hadn't been able to shake the heavy feeling weighing her down.

She silently hoped her dad would be satisfied with small talk for a while. *So, do we think we're going to get any snow? How about those Packers and Vikings?* She wasn't ready to talk about anything else. Not yet.

"I got another e-mail from Josh and Brady already this morning," Patrick informed her cheerfully.

Caitlin wasn't ready to talk about Josh and Brady, either! Or Jenny, who might retreat into her shell again under the barrage of media attention. Or Devon, who had assumed her career meant more than the people she'd come to care about...

What did you expect, Caitlin chided herself. She'd poured her heart and soul into IMAGEine. Of course Devon would assume she wouldn't hesitate to use his family history to feed the fire that kept her business going.

Except that she'd thought they'd both begun to trust each other. Just a little.

"I..." Can't talk about them right now, Dad. If she said that, he'd wonder why. Which would lead to a lot of questions she didn't want to answer. And didn't have answers for. "How is the search going?"

Patrick shot her a shrewd look. "I'll tell you about it on the way to church."

"Church?"

"We still have plenty of time to make the service."

Caitlin hesitated. She wanted to hide, not go to a place guaranteed to peel away the outer layers of her heart and leave them exposed.

As if Patrick could read her mind, he covered her hand with his and gave it a squeeze. "I think of Sunday mornings as my little piece of peace. No matter what I carry in, I leave there feeling lighter."

Peace. There was that word again. Devon had said the same thing—that he'd found peace. Caitlin had always assumed the feeling would automatically accompany a solid reputation and a growing client base. But it hadn't.

And even though she couldn't remember the last time she'd gone to church—had it really been Easter the year before?—she found herself looking forward to attending a worship service.

Over the past few weeks, she'd started a tentative journey to rediscover her faith. She'd spent more time talking to God and she'd even started listening.

Maybe if she followed His steps for a change, she'd find herself on the right path.

"Mr. Walsh?"

Devon found his path blocked by a matchstick of a guy. With hair dyed the color of India ink and enough gold rings in his eyebrows to set off an airport security system.

Definitely not a regular attendee at New Hope Fellowship.

Instantly Devon regretted his decision to take the kids to church. Except that he'd needed to regain his perspective and that wasn't happening in his own head. After a sleepless night and a lot of prayer, he'd reached the conclusion that he was guilty of the very thing he'd accused Caitlin of.

Devon would have pushed past Mr. Metal but Josh and Brady had crowded ahead of him, staring up at the man with extreme fascination.

"Jenny, please take your brothers to the fellowship hall for doughnuts. I'll be there in a few minutes."

Jenny smiled at the stranger, who grinned back as she ushered her brothers away.

The guy extended his hand. "I'm Rob Stafford."

"Leave me and my family alone." Devon took a step forward and found his path blocked again. The guy either liked living dangerously or else he felt safe confronting Devon under the watchful eye of the elderly usher at the end of the aisle.

"I'm not with *Trends,* if that's what you're thinking."

"Sorry, not buying it. If you aren't with *Trends,* then you're with someone else." Devon had heard enough. And it occurred to him that Rob Stafford might have intercepted him so that someone else could approach Jenny and the boys.

"I'm a book reviewer—"

That's all Devon needed to know. Without another word, he pushed past the man and headed up the aisle.

"I'm a friend of Caitlin McBride."

Devon's heart skidded to a stop. He turned around slowly. "I'm listening."

Rob grinned. "Good. Now, did I hear you mention something about doughnuts?"

Chapter Twenty

"That was one of your mother's favorites."

Caitlin, who'd been staring up at the framed sampler over the fireplace, tensed at the sound of her father's voice. She closed her eyes, but it didn't blot out the verse from Proverbs, meticulously captured in blue embroidery floss. The words were already etched in her mind.

> By wisdom a house is built and through understanding it is established. Through knowledge its rooms are filled with rare and beautiful treasures.

"I remember." Its first home had been on the wall of her parent's office. Above Laura's desk. When Caitlin was about ten years old, she'd discovered the wrinkled square of muslin in a box deep in her mother's closet. "I finished it."

"Your mother was thrilled about that." Patrick joined her next to the fireplace. "But do you know the story behind it?"

Caitlin shook her head. If she'd heard the sampler's history at one time, she'd forgotten it. Something else to add to the list.

"After your mother found out that you were on the way, she

started to panic. Apparently she was worried that she wasn't domestic enough to be a good wife and mother. Not when she chased down bad guys for a living and preferred to be outdoors instead of in the kitchen." Patrick chuckled at the memory. "She bought the embroidery kit and worked on it in the evenings. Every time she poked herself with the needle she'd grumble and stick on a bandage, but it made her all the more determined to finish her first decorating project."

"Mom was like that," Caitlin murmured. Determination was a trait Laura had passed on to her oldest daughter.

"When I asked her why she was being so stubborn, she told me that she wanted our home to be beautiful and it was up to her to make it that way. She wanted it to be a place where you could grow and thrive." Patrick's eyes twinkled. "I had to point out the obvious, of course. That you would thrive just because she was your mother—and because she knew how to love even if she never learned how to embroider. She admitted I was right—I always basked in those rare moments, you know—and she laughed, patted her tummy and said 'wouldn't it be something if you were the one who finished it?'"

Caitlin finally understood why Laura's eyes had gotten misty when she'd shown the sampler to her. Her mother wasn't an emotional woman by nature, so the unexpected response had made Caitlin all the more determined to match the little stitches Laura had begun.

The look of approval and pride on her mother's face when she'd shown her the finished work had given Caitlin the confidence to tackle other difficult projects.

Laura had died before Caitlin had graduated from college but her mother's encouragement had spurred on Caitlin to pursue a career that most people didn't understand or even see the value in.

"Caitlin—" The catch in Patrick's voice tugged her attention away from the sampler. When she looked at her father, the moisture gathering in his eyes shocked her. "Is it possible…are you still trying to finish something for your mother?"

The question pierced what remained of the wall around Caitlin's emotions and bits of her past, present and future poured out like debris from a flood.

"I don't understand why she had to die so young, Dad. There was so much she wanted to see. To do."

"Come and sit down, sweetheart." Patrick led her to the sofa and sat down beside her, clasping her hands in his.

"I don't understand, either, but when I trusted God, I decided to trust Him with *everything*. Even the questions I don't have answers for. But I do know this—you can't measure a person's life by the number of days they lived on this earth. You have to look at what they did with those days. I know your mother. She wouldn't have had any regrets about the way she spent hers. She lived her life….and she would want you to live yours."

"But I made a promise…."

"A promise to Mom?"

Caitlin shook her head. "A promise to myself. She always believed in me, Dad. She told me that I could do whatever I set my mind to. Mom wasn't afraid of anything. She was always so confident. So self-assured. I just wanted to be like her. To do something she'd be…proud of."

Patrick's shoulders rose and fell with his sigh. "You don't have to *do* something to make your mother proud of you, sweetheart. She was proud of the person you *are*. And so I am. You've worked hard to achieve your goals but…" Her father paused. "Your mother wouldn't have wanted you to sacrifice love in the process. She knew the treasures in our house weren't the furniture or the china. They weren't the medals or the letters of commendation she got from the mayor. It was our family. You.

Your sisters. Love didn't take anything away from Laura, it made her life *bigger*. That's the legacy she would have wanted to pass on to her daughter."

Caitlin's eyes welled. Her dad was right. She'd been so single-minded over the years, so set on forging her own path she hadn't noticed how narrow it had become. Devon and the children didn't fit neatly into the parameters of her life. Instead, they'd pushed at the boundaries and expanded them. Gave her more room to…grow.

Devon had already learned that lesson. It wasn't that he didn't care that the house needed a coat of paint—he simply cared more about the people living inside of it.

It was part of the reason she'd gone from trying to change him to respecting him. To loving him.

She *loved* Devon.

She loved his flannel shirts and his five o'clock shadow. She loved watching for signs of the half smile that lurked at the corner of his lips. She loved the way he loved his children.

But he'd never trust her again.

"I made a mistake, Dad. I didn't try to, but I did."

Patrick smiled. "That's why they're called mistakes, sweetheart. Because we don't try to make them."

His gentle attempt at humor warmed her. "I don't know what to do."

"About your feelings for Devon?"

Caitlin's mouth fell open. "How did you know?"

Patrick smiled. "Just a lucky guess."

"You can't tell him that I'm here, Dad. Or the kids," Caitlin added in a rush. "I know they've been e-mailing you about the ring and I—"

Patrick patted Caitlin's hand reassuringly, cutting through her panic. "I won't tell them you're here if that's what you want."

What Caitlin wanted was to try on hats with Jenny and

watch the boys pretend to be junior detectives. She wanted to see the tender expression in Devon's eyes when he heard his children laugh. She wanted to stand next to him at the sink, washing dishes in a house where iguanas thought they were dogs and piñatas became family Thanksgiving traditions.

She wanted to be part of Devon's not-so-typical life.

But all she had to do was remember the expression on Devon's face when he'd told her to send a bill for her "time" and she knew it wouldn't happen. Instead, she could only pray that the plan she'd set into motion would minimize the damages Dawn Gallagher could potentially inflict.

Was she being a coward by hiding out in Cooper's Landing? Shirking her responsibilities? She'd never been a quitter before.

"I should drive back before it gets any later." Even though she felt…battle weary. Weighted down from wrestling with the past and having to face a future that had somehow eluded her best attempt to control it.

"You know," Patrick mused. "Even Jesus took time away from His ministry to be alone. To pray and to rest."

He'd read her mind. And she made up hers.

"Do you mind…can I stay here a few days?"

Patrick pressed a kiss to her temple. "You can stay as long as you'd like."

"You may regret that offer. I might not want to go back."

"Then you'll have to go forward."

"Dad—" Caitlin choked back a laugh. "You are as optimistic as Meghan. Sometimes things don't work out the way you…planned."

"That's why it's comforting to know that God has a plan." Patrick winked at her.

After Caitlin thought about that for a moment, she realized it was.

* * *

"Dad?"

Devon heard Jenny's voice behind him and silently braced himself for the question he knew was about to come.

He turned away from the computer screen—the blank computer screen—and scraped up a smile. "What's up?"

"I heard the phone ring. Was it Caitlin?"

"No." Devon wished it had been. "Her assistant said she'd taken some time off, remember?"

Jenny looked confused and he knew exactly what his daughter was thinking. Caitlin and vacations went together like Caitlin and being late.

He didn't believe it, either, but even a stare-down contest with Sabrina Buckley the day before hadn't yielded any success. He'd gone to Caitlin's office to see her, only to be informed that Caitlin had taken some time off.

Devon had schmoozed his way around Sabrina before but this time she refused to cooperate. All she could tell him was that Caitlin had left a message, asking her to reschedule her appointments for the week and that she'd be in touch. By the time Devon left, he actually believed that Sabrina had no idea where Caitlin was, either.

Devon's only consolation was knowing Caitlin had been in touch with *someone*. Whenever he tried to call her cell phone, it immediately went to voice mail. He'd left several messages at her apartment and even added his own addendum to an e-mail Josh sent to Patrick McBride, dropping a strong hint to Caitlin's father that he was anxious to talk to Caitlin and if he knew where she was, could he ask her to call?

So far, all his efforts had been in vain. And he had no one to blame but himself.

Jenny shifted from foot to foot. "But if she's on vacation, she could still call."

"She will." Devon had to believe that no matter how much he'd damaged their relationship, she'd keep her promise to his daughter.

Jenny's expression brightened a little at the confidence in his voice. "Good. Because I found a Mexican restaurant in the yellow pages we can—"

"Dad!" Josh and Brady's excited shrieks drowned their sister out. "Come down here. *Quick.*"

The boys, Devon thought with a shake of his head, had definitely bounced back after their ear infections.

He followed Jenny downstairs to the foyer, where Josh and Brady bounced on either side of Rob Stafford like matching pogo sticks while Rosie ran circles around them.

"When I saw the gate around your place, I was afraid you'd have a Doberman guarding the door." Rob grinned as he bent down to pet Rosie, who promptly flipped over and exposed her belly for a scratch.

Devon rolled his eyes. And grinned back. Spiked hair and piercings aside, the guy was growing on him.

During their conversation over doughnuts that day, Rob said he'd met Caitlin at Daybreak, a country getaway for women in remission from cancer where she worked as a volunteer. Rob had arrived a few minutes early to pick up his wife, Zoey, after a weekend retreat and found her and Caitlin standing on a makeshift stage, performing for the talent show. Rob, who hadn't heard his wife laugh since her hair had started falling out, saw Zoey playing air guitar while Caitlin belted out an out-of-tune version of a popular eighties song.

Another facet, Devon had thought, of the woman he'd once dismissed as being only concerned with outward appearance. And another reason to apologize.

If he could *find* her.

"So, are you ready to make your bow into society, dude?" Rob asked.

Like he was ready for surgery without an anesthetic, Devon thought.

Brady made a face. "Dad has to bow?"

"It's a figure of speech, Brady Bunch."

"Brady who?"

"That was a little before their time," Devon pointed out mildly. "They aren't a product of the seventies, you know." Neither was Rob, but he'd embraced the era anyway. In fact, the guy was a walking collage of *several* eras.

"Then they should watch more cable."

Devon handed out coats and watched his children dash out the door and down to the curb where Rob's classic VW bus, painted an eye-popping shade of Do-Not-Cross-Police-Line yellow, had planted two of its wheels.

"Sorry I didn't bring the limo."

Devon didn't smile. And when he reached for his coat, his hand froze on the hanger as ice-cold panic sluiced through his veins.

Am I doing the right thing, God?

It was a question he'd been asking repeatedly over the past few days. And so far, he hadn't received a response. Did that mean he should wait?

"Dev." Rob cuffed him lightly on the shoulder. "We can still cancel, man. No worries. If you're not ready, you're not ready."

Devon met Rob's earnest gaze as he offered a last minute escape route. It might have been difficult for Devon to wrap his head around *some* things but it didn't take a genius to figure out that Zoey's medical bills had to be pinching the couples' bank accounts. Hard.

Caitlin had had a twofold reason for sending Rob to him. And Devon couldn't back out at this point any more than he could let a certain image consultant get away.

"Let's go." He shot Rob a rueful smile. "Maybe no one will show."

"Dude." Rob raised a pierced brow. "You have a wicked sense of humor."

"I wasn't kidding."

Rob just shook his head and laughed.

Chapter Twenty-One

Caitlin wandered into the living room and paused in front of the window to watch the snowflakes fall. Lake-effect snow, her dad called it, but the scientific-sounding term didn't do justice to the haze of fluffy, silver-blue snowflakes that filled the air and made her feel as if she were walking around inside of a snow globe.

Patrick had gone over to his friend Jacob Cutter's house to supposedly drop off something but Caitlin hadn't been fooled by the excuse. He was giving her time alone to think.

The trouble was, thinking *hurt* at the moment. So she'd put on her sweats, made a cup of tea and let the peaceful silence spread like a balm over her soul as she talked to God about the future.

And the past.

She'd tried so hard to be like her mother—strong and confident—and yet she'd completely forgotten the *source* of Laura's confidence. Her faith in God.

Instead of honoring her mother's life, the goals Caitlin strived to achieve had taken on a life of their own. She'd unwittingly let them crowd out the thing Laura had held most dear. People. Relationships.

Which drew Caitlin's thoughts irresistibly back to Devon.

He might not trust her, but hopefully he'd see the wisdom in the plan she'd set into motion....

The antique telephone on the coffee table rattled to life and Caitlin hesitated, not certain she should answer it. Devon had left several messages and she hadn't returned his calls. With her shields down, Caitlin wasn't ready to expose her heart for target practice.

She reached for the phone, reminding herself that Devon wouldn't bother tracking her to her father's home in Cooper's Landing.

No matter how much she wished otherwise.

"McBride residence."

"Caitlin, it's Dad."

She frowned at the odd inflection in Patrick's voice. "Are you okay?"

"Are you...watching the news?"

Caitlin glanced at the blank television screen. "No."

"You might want to. Watch the news. Ah, *now*."

"Dad, what's—"

Click.

Her father had hung up on her.

Caitlin shook off the afghan she'd wrapped around her bare feet and crossed the room to turn the television on.

And found herself looking right into Devon's eyes.

Caitlin's knees buckled and she sat down hard on her backside as she listened to the anchor's cheerful voice-over.

"Young adult author D. Birch made a surprising guest appearance at Wing Tips Bookstore in Minneapolis this morning, much to the delight of his devoted fans. Birch writes the popular Ransom mystery series and is here to sign copies of his latest release, which won't be available in other stores until mid-December.

"Birch is a pen name for Devon Walsh, who, unbeknownst to the public until this morning, has resided in the Twin Cities area for almost six years.

"Birch's identity has been as full of mystery as the plots for his books. When asked why he decided to step out in the spotlight, Birch said only that he had 'three very good reasons.' And although he didn't reveal what those reasons were, his fans don't seem to mind if he maintains a little bit of mystery—they're just glad he's here."

Caitlin covered her mouth with her hand as she watched Devon smile and autograph one of his books for a teenage boy.

Rob Stafford stood like a sentinel behind Devon's shoulder, his stance protective rather than an attempt to garner a share of the attention.

"Thanks, Rob," Caitlin whispered.

She'd known the men would get along.

The camera panned the interior of the bookstore and paused briefly on one of the round tables, where Josh, Brady and Jenny sat with Rob's wife, Zoey.

The twins grinned and flapped their hands at the camera while Jenny flashed a shy smile before ducking her head. A sweetly familiar gesture that brought an instant knot to Caitlin's throat.

She held her breath, waiting for the anchor to comment on the children and Devon's former marriage to fashion model Ashleigh Heath.

Birch will be at Wing Tips until three o'clock for those of you who want to meet the author. Back to you, Margaret.

Caitlin toppled over and rolled onto her back, grinning up at the ceiling.

It had worked.

* * *

"Mmm. Do I smell garlic?" Patrick paused in the kitchen doorway and sniffed the air appreciatively as Caitlin flitted around the kitchen, looking for a colander.

She paused mid-flit. "Yes, you do. I'm making dinner."

Spaghetti. Not because she was feeling nostalgic...because she *liked* it.

"It smells wonderful. I didn't know you were such an accomplished chef."

A few days ago, Caitlin would have simply nodded in agreement. But now the innocent comment arrowed through her, reminding her of something else she'd missed.

"You should come to The Cities for a few weeks, Dad," she said impulsively. "You could close up right before Christmas and stay with me until Easter if you wanted to. Visit Meghan and Cade. Hang out with Mr. Darcy."

Patrick cleared his throat. "That's a very tempting offer. Cooper's Landing does quiet down until the ice thaws."

Definitely an understatement. The little town on the Lake Superior shore practically went into hibernation!

"Just think about it. We haven't had a Christmas together since..." Caitlin tried to retrieve the most recent one from her memory file. And failed.

That's how long it had been.

December was one of her busiest months at IMAGEine. Every year, more often than not, she ended up plugging any empty holes in her calendar with family members as close to Christmas Day as possible in order to satisfy the holiday-visit requirements.

"I have a nice guest room." Which, Caitlin realized, no one had ever stayed in. When Evie came to The Cities, she stayed with Meghan. Caitlin had never understood why. Her sister's neighborhood wasn't exactly a gated community, unless a person counted the bars on the first floor windows of the apartment building!

I'm sorry, Lord.

What had she thought? That she could put her family aside in much the same way she'd put God aside while she'd pursued her goals? God's steadfast faithfulness had been reflected in her family—they'd loved her even when she hadn't been all that loveable.

"I'll have Christmas this year," Caitlin said firmly. "I'll invite Evie and Sam, too."

Memories crowded in. Turkey piñatas and jigsaw puzzles and feeling the gentle strength of Devon's hand holding hers while he prayed before dinner.

What crazy traditions would he add to make his first Christmas with the children special? Would they still be living with him at Christmas?

She'd managed to displace the media attention from Jenny but would Devon end up losing custody anyway? The court hearing was scheduled for some time in December but he hadn't told her the exact date....

"Caitlin? I think something is burning."

Caitlin whirled toward the oven and rushed to open the door. Smoke poured out, revealing the charcoaled remains of the garlic bread.

Her eyes watered—and not only from the smoke. "I guess I'm not the accomplished chef you thought I was."

"You are still an accomplished chef," Patrick said. "All this means is that you're an accomplished chef who occasionally burns the garlic bread. Don't be so hard on yourself, Caitlin Rae. I think the only person who demands perfection from you is *you*."

Caitlin Rae. Her father hadn't called her that since she was about…Jenny's age. When the pairing of her first and middle name generally popped up in a lecture—or what her parents had preferred to call teachable moments.

"I love you, Dad." Caitlin couldn't remember the last time she'd said the words.

Patrick's eyes widened and Caitlin winced inwardly. It must have been a while.

"I love you, too, sweetheart." Patrick tossed her a pot holder. And a sly wink. "Do you mind if we eat in the den? I could use your help."

A red flag popped up. The only thing in Patrick's den was his computer. A computer that linked him to trouble. "With what?" she asked suspiciously.

"I remember you were always good at solving puzzles."

"Puzzles or mysteries?"

"That," her father answered cheerfully, "depends entirely on your point of view."

"Dad, you are…amazing." Caitlin blinked at the spread-sheet Patrick put down in front of her. "How did you come up with all this in such a short time?"

Her father's cheeks reddened. "It's called retirement."

Or, Caitlin thought in exasperation, an obsession. Still, she couldn't help but be impressed.

"A local lumberjack told me that if the bark had grown around the ring the way you'd described, he guestimated it might have been put there at least twenty-five years ago. Possibly longer," Patrick explained. "I traced the family names of the last three owners in that time period and came up with Wickert, Fisher and Rush. Not an *L* in the bunch, as you can see. For all we know, a visitor could have carved those initials in the tree. Maybe a babysitter. Who knows?"

Caitlin picked up a pen and drew a rough sketch of the heart from memory, filling in the initials of their mystery lovers.

"I did a search of Wickerts—they lived in the house in the mid-sixties to late seventies—but I haven't put together a complete call list yet. They'd definitely fall within the time frame, though."

Caitlin idly drew another heart farther down on the sheet of paper as she watched her father pace the floor and talk through several possible scenarios out loud.

"What are you doing?" Patrick stopped abruptly behind her.

"Noth—" Caitlin gulped. In the center of the heart, she'd drawn two initials: *C* and *D*.

Are you in junior high? she wailed silently.

"*C* and *D*." Patrick stared down at the paper. When she would have scribbled it out—in utter humiliation—he plucked the pen out of her hand.

And started to laugh.

"Dad!"

"I didn't even *think* of that." Patrick's eyes lit with excitement. "*C*—Caitlin. Most people would naturally put their own initial first, before someone else's. And *D*—Devon—" Patrick ignored her sputter of denial. "Your first initial, his first initial. I assumed someone had carved the first and last initials of the person he or she loved. Not a combination of two *first* names. Caitlin, you're a genius. I've been concentrating on family names—last names—when I should have been researching full names."

"You can…find that out?"

Patrick's eyes sparkled. "My dear daughter, finding things is what I do best."

Caitlin found herself caught in a whirlwind. She and her sisters had always lovingly referred to their father as the absent-minded professor but after two hours of complicated Internet searches that ended in an organized contact list, she had to admit he had a gift.

They started with the Wickerts, the name of the earliest owners Patrick had found.

"No good. Bernard Wickert and his wife, Carol, were the only ones living in the house." Caitlin put a line through their name.

"We could go back a little further. They may be able to tell us who they bought the house from. Let's see if we can find them." Patrick's fingers flew over the keyboard. "Houston, Texas. Here's the number."

Caitlin's mouth fell open. "You're scary, Dad."

"Not bad for a retired English teacher, mmm?" Patrick busied himself with his own search while Caitlin dialed the number, praying the Wickerts wouldn't think she was trying to sell them a condo…or steal their identity.

She needn't have worried. Bernard Wickert answered the phone and it quickly became clear the man could have kept up a lively conversation with a statue!

"The homeowner found some property on the premises and we're trying to trace it back to its original owner," Caitlin explained carefully. "It has a…monogram…on it. An *A* and an *L*."

"We bought the house from a man named Gil Martin. Had to do everything long distance, though, because he moved his family to Arkansas or Arizona. Felt sorry for the guy—lost his son in Nam and took it pretty hard. His wife said he couldn't stand the memories so they loaded up lock, stock and barrel and moved out. We had to wait to move in, though, 'cause they'd rented the house out for the summer…"

"Rented it out?" Caitlin interrupted.

"Lots of upheaval back then." Bernard sighed.

"Do you remember their name?" Caitlin didn't know why, but a dozen butterflies took wing in her stomach.

"Nope, can't recollect the name. Sorry."

Caitlin tamped down her disappointment. "Thank you for your time, Mr. Wickert."

"Oh, time is all I've got, young lady. Call back again if you have a mind to."

Caitlin smiled and hung up the phone, aware that her father had stopped working to tune in on the conversation. She relayed the information and Patrick held out a piece of paper.

"I expanded the search and found the name of the neighbors who lived next door for the last fifty years. They moved out about ten years ago but someone might remember the name of the family who'd rented that summer."

Caitlin glanced at the clock. "It's almost nine, Dad. Shouldn't we wait until tomorrow?"

"This will be the last one," Patrick said. "It's your area code, so go ahead and do the honors. You seem to be on a roll."

Caitlin shook her head and punched in the numbers. Someone picked up the phone almost immediately. "Is this the Kent residence?"

"Yesss."

"Please don't hang up." The hesitation in the woman's voice warned Caitlin that she better be quick or she'd be talking to dead air. She launched into a brief explanation as to why she was calling and then got to the crux of the matter. "I'm hoping you can connect me with a member of the Kent family who'd lived in that neighborhood."

"I did. I grew up there."

Caitlin couldn't believe it. The rush of adrenaline she felt gave her a new understanding as to why her father enjoyed his hobby. "Do you happen to remember the name of a family that rented the house next door before the Wickerts moved in?"

"Their name was…Jansen." The words barely broke above a whisper.

"Jansen." Caitlin jotted down the name. "Thank you. That should help—"

"What did you say this was about?" Ms. Kent interrupted.

"Some property was discovered on the premises recently and

we believe it's been there a long time. It's rather valuable, so we're trying to locate the owner."

Silence.

"Ms. Kent?" Had she hung up?

"Ms. Kent makes me feel like I'm back in the classroom teaching Shakespeare again. Please, call me Leona."

Chapter Twenty-Two

Caitlin stared down at the heart she'd drawn on the piece of paper. No, she pushed the thought aside; it had to be a coincidence. They'd found the ring in a tree in Devon's yard, not the Kents' next door.

"Ah, *Leona,* do you remember the…first names of the Jansen family?"

"Rachel and Paul were the parents."

"They had children, then. Do you remember their names?"

"I don't know why you're looking for them. The family didn't have much money—I can't imagine they left anything valuable behind."

Caitlin drew in a breath, surprised by the sudden defensiveness in the woman's tone. "We don't know if the property belongs to the Jansens or someone else. My friends—the people who live in the house now—just want to see it returned to its rightful owner."

"Anthony," Leona said softly. "They had a son named Anthony."

Caitlin stared down at the *A* she'd written on the paper and her heart started to pound. "How old was Anthony Jansen that summer?"

"Nineteen."

"And how old were…you?" Caitlin's fingers tightened around the pen in her hand.

"I don't see the relevance of that," Leona said, the quaver back in her voice.

Caitlin waited.

"Eighteen. And I think you have all the information you need now—"

"Ms. Kent, please don't hang up," Caitlin said quickly. "The boys who live in the house now found a heart carved in the willow tree in the backyard. Did Anthony do it?"

"What could that possibly have to do with property found in the house?"

"Because we didn't find the property in the house. We found it hidden in the trunk of the tree underneath the initials. *Your* initials." Caitlin decided she wouldn't get anywhere if she didn't tell the truth. "It was a ring, Ms. Kent. Is it possible it was meant for you?"

Caitlin could almost *feel* the woman's shock.

"Was it…a diamond in the center of a gold braid?"

Now it was Caitlin's turn to be shocked, even though she'd already guessed Leona had been the intended recipient of the ring. "You saw it?"

"No—but Anthony told me about it. The ring was a family heirloom. His grandmother had willed it to him to give to his future bride, but I can't believe he—" Leona's voice ebbed away.

"Gave it to you," Caitlin finished.

"We hadn't known each other very long, but it felt…long enough. We fell in love that summer and talked about a future together. The war was going on and Tony… He enlisted. I was so angry that he'd made that decision. I told him that I didn't want to wait to start our future together. When he asked me to meet him by the tree the night before he left, I thought he wanted to say goodbye. I didn't show up—I knew I was being stubborn, but I needed time to think, so I went to stay with my sister. When I came back, his family was gone. And so was Tony."

"He didn't contact you?"

"No. My parents were right. What Tony and I had…it was a summer romance. He promised me that we'd be together, but it hadn't meant anything." Leona paused and drew a shaky breath.

"A month after he left, my mother said she'd heard a rumor that Tony was…missing in action. I never saw or heard from him again."

Missing in action.

Caitlin sucked in a breath. "I'm so sorry."

"It was a long time ago. A lifetime, really."

The thread of wistfulness in the words told Caitlin that while the logical side of Leona's brain counted the years that had passed; her heart persisted in counting the memories.

Was it going to be like this with Devon, Caitlin wondered. Was she going to think about him years from now? Would she move forward with her heart trapped in a time capsule, dated the day she'd fallen in love with him?

Maybe it would have been better if she hadn't let herself get close to him…

"Please tell your friend that if he can't find Tony's parents, to please sell the ring and give the money to charity," Leona was saying.

Caitlin didn't know if it was fair to put the woman through additional pain, but maybe the diamond would provide some sort of closure to a chapter of her life that Leona hadn't closed, no matter what she claimed to the contrary. "Don't you want to see the ring? It's beautiful—and there's an inscription on the band."

"Tony never mentioned an inscription. What did it say?"

"I can't remember." Not the *exact* words anyway. "He wanted you to have the ring, Leona. Shouldn't you at least *see* it?"

"Do you think your friends would mind?"

"The boys who found it would love to meet you in person. They've been so anxious to find you."

"I'll see the ring on one condition."

Caitlin couldn't help but grin. "Great. What's the condition?"

"That you come with me."

"It's pretty cold out here—if you're that desperate for a story, you should have dressed for the weather."

The woman standing near the front gate visibly started at the sound of Devon's voice.

He'd been leaving the gate unlocked for the past few days—not wanting anything to deter Caitlin if she decided to come back. He'd also formed a habit of looking out the window every half hour or so for the very same reason. That's how he happened to see a woman standing almost motionless just inside the fence, her attention focused on the house.

When he'd checked a few minutes later, she was still there. Devon was half tempted to let her stand there and freeze—but it would bring another round of publicity to his door, not to mention be a poor witness for his faith.

That's when he decided to let them know that Sunny the iguana was better at blending into the environment!

"Devon?" A faint but familiar voice drifted back in response to his greeting.

Devon tossed a look over his shoulder to see if the kids were close by before he grabbed his coat and stumbled down the steps.

The woman met him halfway.

"What are you doing here, Vickie?"

His sister-in-law's teeth chattered. "I was t-trying to get up the nerve to come to the door to talk to you."

Devon was tempted to remind her that the last time they'd spoken, Vickie had said that any further conversations would take place between their attorneys.

It couldn't be a coincidence that she'd turned up just days before the custody hearing.

"I'll only take up a few minutes of your time. Please, Dev."

Looking down at his former sister-in-law, Devon felt an unexpected rush of compassion. Vickie had never been as strikingly beautiful as Ashleigh but now her cheeks looked hollow and dark circles shadowed her eyes. Ashleigh's death had not only taken an emotional toll on her but also a physical one.

"Come inside the house where it's warm."

To his surprise, Vickie shook her head. "I don't want the children to see me."

For the first time, Devon noticed a car parked down the block with its engine running, far enough away that he could barely make out the features of the person sitting in the driver's seat.

"Okay, tell me what's going on?"

"I'm dropping the custody suit," Vickie said quietly.

Devon's heart stalled and there was a sudden rushing noise in his ears. "Dropping it?" he repeated, not believing he'd actually heard her right.

"I can't do this to them. To Jenny." Her voice shook but Devon had the feeling it wasn't due to the cold. "That lifestyle is too crazy."

A chill snaked its way up Devon's spine as his suspicions returned. "Can't what? Turn Jenny into her mother?"

Vickie didn't deny that that had been her plan. "A friend got through to me…convinced me to go into a treatment center. I'm leaving tomorrow morning."

A treatment center. Devon tried not to recoil but Vickie must have seen something in his eyes.

"Not drugs, Dev. Although I have to admit those were always

available, too." She gave him a broken smile. "I'm anorexic. I told myself that I had things under control—that all I needed was to get back on my feet again after Ash died. I needed a reason."

"Jenny." Devon closed his eyes briefly.

"We get along. She's a great kid—not the diva that Ashleigh could be sometimes. I thought I'd be doing her a favor to get her into the business. Give her the world." Vickie bit her lip. "I…changed my mind. I don't want her in *that* world. Not anymore. And my friend told me that I can't use the kids as a reason to get better. *I* have to be the reason I want to get better."

Devon was torn. Torn between compassion for Vickie's struggle and anger that she'd hidden the truth from him.

Compassion won.

He opened his arms and Vickie stepped into them. She didn't cry, just stood still with her face buried against his chest as if the conversation had totally drained her of emotion.

Devon felt the slightness of her frame under the bulky coat and winced.

"You must think I'm a terrible person," Vickie whispered.

"I think you're brave to admit you need help," Devon said. And he meant it. "Are you sure you don't want to come in and say hello? The kids would love to see you."

Vickie stepped away and thrust her hands in her coat pockets. "It would be too hard right now. I can't have contact with family members for the first stage of my treatment, but after that…I would like to keep in touch. If you don't mind."

"I don't mind," he told her. "And, Vic? I'll be praying for you."

"Thanks. I could use all the help I can get." Vickie started to walk away but before she reached the gate, she looked back. "Dev? Ashleigh thought she was doing the right thing with the kids, but before she died she mentioned that maybe they should spend more time with you. I think the pressure was making her think about things in a different way. I just wish…" Her voice trailed off and she shrugged. "I won't threaten to take Jenny and the boys away again. Ever. And for what it's worth, I'm sorry I put you through this. I know they'll be happy with you."

It's worth a lot, Devon thought.

By the time Vickie stepped through the gate, the car had pulled alongside the curb and the driver, a man with graying hair and steady eyes, lifted his hand in a brief salute as she climbed in.

Devon had the feeling that he was Vickie's friend—the one who'd convinced her to go into treatment.

The car pulled away and Devon stood in the yard, numbed by the reality of what had just happened. God had answered his prayers again—they didn't have to go through the stress of another custody battle. And thanks to Caitlin, the press was more interested in D. Birch than Devon Walsh's twelve-year-old daughter.

Caitlin.

He wanted to call her and share the news about Vickie. He wanted to be able to share a lot of things with her. Laughter. Love. *Life.*

Devon looked up at the flurries swirling above his head.

Thank you for answering my prayers about the custody hearing in a way I never imagined that you would. Thank you that Vickie is seeking help and I have my children back for good. But God? I hope you don't mind if I ask for one more thing.

Chapter Twenty-Three

"**D**ad, don't freak but there's a lady at the door." Brady, resembling an astronaut in snow pants and a down parka, appeared in the kitchen doorway. A puddle immediately formed around his boots as the heat from the kitchen melted the snow on them.

The first winter storm had hit the Twin Cities area the day before, dumping eight inches of moist, heavy snow on the ground. Devon had spent the morning constructing forts, dodging snowballs and shoveling paths to the mailbox and the garage.

He'd finally taken a break to make lunch while the children stayed outside to play.

"A reporter?" There'd been a few of those over the past week but thanks to Rob Stafford, even their interest had been dwindling. He should almost be offended—if he weren't so relieved.

"I don't think so." Brady's shrug dislodged a miniature avalanche of snow. "Just a lady."

A lady. But not the one Devon wanted to see. That particular lady had turned off her cell phone, shut down her laptop and taken an unscheduled "vacation."

Now Caitlin decided to be impulsive.

His hope lay in the fact that it was Saturday—and Caitlin had told Sabrina to expect her back Monday morning.

Devon planned to be her first appointment of the day.

He turned down the burner under a kettle of sloppy Joe sauce and reached for a dish towel to wipe his hands on. When he stepped into the hallway, he almost bumped into a petite elderly woman. Brady was right—she didn't *look* like a reporter. Auburn streaked her silver hair and lively green eyes smiled up at him.

Devon blinked. "I'm sorry. I didn't see you."

"I'm the one who should be apologizing for barging in like this. Your children said I'd find you in here."

"Do I...know you?"

"I'm Leona Kent." Leona laughed again when she saw his blank expression. "I've been told you found something that might belong to me."

Devon didn't even try to hide his surprise. "Patrick found you?"

"Patrick McBride?" Leona tilted her head and a thoughtful look entered her eyes. "Yes—I suppose Patrick can take some of the credit. He is a very determined man."

"Yes, well, it runs in the family," Devon muttered. "Please, come in. I'll get the kids—I know they'll want to meet you."

"They said they'd be right in." Leona smiled again and started to walk down the hall to the parlor.

As if she knew exactly where it was.

Devon followed, feeling a little unnerved by the unexpected visitor. Josh and Brady had received an e-mail from Caitlin's father that hinted he'd had a breakthrough in his search for the ring's owner but he hadn't expected that breakthrough to show up at his door!

"Can I get you something to drink? Coffee? Tea?" Devon scraped up long-forgotten hospitality skills as Leona settled comfortably into one of the chairs that didn't have a pile of folded laundry on it.

"I'm fine." Leona's expression turned pensive as she looked around the room. "It doesn't look that different."

Devon rested a hip against the sofa, his curiosity trumping caution. "Did you live here?"

"I grew up in the white house next door. My parents lived there fifty years. My father passed away almost ten years ago and my mother moved into assisted living."

Devon winced as the front door slammed and his children's laughter echoed through the house. Followed by a stampede of feet down the hall.

"Three…two…" Devon counted, aware of Leona Kent's amusement.

The twins exploded into the room, eyes shining and cheeks ruddy from the cold.

"Boys, no running in the house," Devon said automatically as their stocking feet hit the hardwood floor and they skidded toward him, propelled by sheer momentum alone.

"Sorry!" They leveled identical grins at their visitor, instantly charming her.

"Where is Jenny?" Devon knew the whole family should be there to hear what Leona Kent had to say.

"I'm right here, Dad," his daughter sang out as she came into the room.

With Caitlin at her side.

She looked beautiful. Softer, somehow. She'd traded in her usual business attire for a black sweater and a pair of faded jeans that accentuated her long legs and subtle curves.

He took a step forward and realized he couldn't exactly pull her into his arms and kiss her senseless in front of an audience. But it didn't stop him from *wanting* to.

"Hello, Devon." She gave him the barest of smiles as Jenny

took her hand and led her into the room. As if now that Caitlin had finally arrived, Jenny wasn't going to let her get away again.

I'm with you, sweetheart, Devon thought.

Because he didn't trust himself not to give into his first inclination, Devon kept his distance. But not for long. If God had given him an opportunity to make it clear to Caitlin how he felt about her, he wasn't going to pass it up.

"I insisted that Caitlin accompany me here today," Leona said. "I'm sure I would have lost my nerve and not shown up if she hadn't. It's hard to face the past…and mistakes you've made."

The sorrow in the Leona's eyes convinced Devon that she was the person who could explain how the ring had ended up lodged in his willow tree. "I'll be right back."

When he returned a few moments later, Josh and Brady had crowded as close to Leona as possible while Jenny and Caitlin sat together on the couch. Caitlin averted her eyes when he walked past and Devon felt a stab of frustration. As much as he wanted to hear what Leona had to say, he wanted to talk to Caitlin alone even more.

Without ceremony, Devon opened his fingers so Leona could see the jewelry cradled in his palm.

"Oh.…" Leona caught her breath and tears leaked out of the corners of her eyes. "I don't know how Tony…I never dreamed he was going to propose that night."

Now Caitlin did look at him, her eyes full of compassion.

"Do you mind telling us what happened, Leona?"

She shook her head and haltingly began to tell them about the summer she'd fallen in love with a young man her parents hadn't approved of.

"Tony's parents rented the house for the summer while they raised money for the mission field. My father didn't understand—he questioned their motivation and said that asking for financial support was like accepting charity. They didn't want us spending time together but we couldn't help it. We fell in love but Tony hadn't told me that he wanted to enlist. When I found out, I was afraid he'd never come back. My mother found me almost hysterical that afternoon and suggested I go away for a few days. Tony had asked me to meet him that night by the tree but I didn't—I went to my sister's instead. By the time I came back, Tony had left. He'd promised we'd be together but he must not have loved me as much as I loved him."

"I don't think that's true," Caitlin said. "You said that Anthony hadn't mentioned an inscription in the band of his grandmother's ring—maybe that was something he'd added just for you."

Leona turned the ring toward the light and squinted at the tiny lettering on the inside of the band. "1 Cor. 13:7. I don't know what that means."

"It's a verse out of the first book of Corinthians," Devon explained.

"But what does it say?"

"I'll get my Bible." Jenny was up in a flash and came back with a pink leather-bound book. She sat beside Leona and flipped through the pages. "I found it." Jenny glanced at Leona and the woman nodded, giving her permission to read it out loud. "It always protects, always trusts, always hopes, always perseveres."

"It's talking about love," Caitlin said. "I think that's why Tony left the ring. He was hoping you'd find it and that you'd know it meant he was coming back for you."

Leona's face lost its color and Devon put a bracing hand on her shoulder. She clung to him and the anguish in her eyes told him the end of the story.

"Did he come back?" Josh asked innocently.

"I heard that he...disappeared during the war." As if she couldn't resist the impulse, Leona slipped the ring on her finger.

It fit perfectly.

"My father is still looking for the Jansens," Caitlin said, her voice husky. "But until he finds them, maybe you should keep the ring."

"I agree," Devon said. "Anthony wanted you to have it."

"I don't deserve it." Leona stared at the diamond. "I was childish and stubborn. I punished him for sticking to his values—the same ones I'd fallen in love with—because I didn't want him to leave. I wish I would have…believed him."

"Let's give Ms. Kent a few minutes alone, guys," Devon suggested.

"Thank you, but I should be going." Leona stood up, her smile as fragile as glass.

"We didn't mean to make you sad," Josh said worriedly.

"You didn't make me sad," Leona assured him. "I'm glad you boys found the ring. I'd always wondered…."

Caitlin rose to her feet. "Would you like me to drive you home?"

"It's not necessary." For the first time, a faint sparkle returned to Leona's eyes. "Stay here and visit with your friends awhile. Thank you for agreeing to come with me, Caitlin, but I can find my way home from here."

Caitlin linked her arm through Leona's. "I'll walk you out."

Devon sank into a chair as the two women left the room and tried to straighten out his own tangled thoughts. One small decision made in anger had changed the course of two people's lives. Forever.

He wasn't about to let that happen to him and Caitlin.

"Dad?" Jenny tugged at his arm.

"What is it, hon?"

Jenny gave an exasperated huff. "If you don't stop Caitlin, she's going to leave again."

Devon grabbed his daughter, kissed her on the cheek and lunged to his feet.

Jenny was right.

By the time he skidded out the front door, Caitlin was almost to the gate.

"Caitlin. Wait."

No, no, no. She couldn't face Devon right now.

But he caught up to her before she reached the gate. She whirled around and tried to keep her face expressionless. "Yes?"

Devon didn't look the least bit intimidated. In fact, the man had the audacity to *smile* at her.

"You can't keep running away from us."

"There is no 'us.'"

"I disagree. And I'll prove it. Come with me." Devon scraped his fingers through his hair when she didn't move. "Please."

She gave in. Reluctantly.

Devon bypassed the shoveled sidewalk, dragging her through the snow and around the corner of the house, where he stopped abruptly. "Look at that and tell me there is no *us*."

The children had made snowmen. But not ordinary snowmen, Caitlin realized. These were snowpeople. Five of them. Three smallish ones—two wearing felt fedoras and identical pairs of black sunglasses while the other modeled a long pink scarf and matching hat. The snowman towering above them had a garish tie around his neck.

Caitlin's gaze moved to the last one in the group. A snow-*woman*. She wore a "pearl" necklace made out of gravel and the ugliest purse Caitlin had ever seen dangled from her "stick" arm.

"They did this all on their own," Devon murmured. "Because they know you belong here. With us. With *me*."

Caitlin couldn't answer around the lump in her throat. She *wasn't* going to cry. She absolutely wasn't.

"Why did you leave, Cait?"

"Because you thought I'd teamed up with Dawn to get to Jenny." It hurt Caitlin to say the words out loud. "And why wouldn't you believe it?" she added softly.

"Why wouldn't I?" Devon repeated. "Because you are an amazing, generous woman. A woman who cares about Jenny and makes her smile again. I know you didn't have an agenda, Cait, because I know *you*."

"But when I brought Jenny home from the mall that day—"

"I overreacted," Devon interrupted swiftly. "I was a dad who wasn't ready to admit his daughter is growing up. In a few years she's going to be as beautiful as her mother and I let my fears get in the way. Once I cleared my head, I tried to tell you that I trusted you, but you ran away."

"I didn't run away," Caitlin muttered. "I...planned a new direction."

Devon suppressed a smile. "I was planning a trip to Cooper's Landing if you didn't show up for work on Monday."

She didn't answer. *Couldn't* answer.

"Cait? Are you crying?"

"I never cry." She sniffled. "I'm just giving my emotions an escape hatch."

Devon took a risk and slipped his arm around Caitlin's waist. She stiffened and then leaned against him, the top of her silky hair brushing his chin. For a moment, he closed his eyes, content to simply breathe in the scent of her. "After listening to Leona's story, I realized I have too many regrets from the past. I couldn't let you walk out the door and be one more."

"I know all about regrets, too." Caitlin met his gaze and Devon saw his reflection in the tears pooling in her eyes. What he saw there gave him hope.

But he couldn't resist teasing her a little. "The snowman is a pretty good likeness but I'm wondering if maybe he shouldn't ditch that loud tie. It's not exactly going to impress the lady."

"I think," Caitlin murmured. "The lady is very impressed. And she wouldn't change a thing."

"Really?" A slow smile spread across Devon's face.

"Really."

His eyes darkened. The words somehow didn't seem big enough to describe his feelings but he said them anyway. "I love you, Cait."

"I thought authors are supposed to *show* not *tell,* Mr. Birch," Caitlin teased him back.

Devon smiled, and with his children cheering loudly from the window, took her in his arms and showed her.

Epilogue

"Not so fast."

Caitlin gave a little yelp as Devon caught her as she swept past him with a smile on her way to the kitchen. He smelled like fresh air and evergreen, compliments of the enormous balsam they'd spent the morning decorating.

"They're going to be here any minute and I still have a million things to do," Caitlin protested. Too bad she didn't sound very convincing.

"Is kissing me one of the million things you have to do?" Devon raised an eyebrow.

Caitlin smiled. "Actually, that just moved to the top of the list."

"I was hoping you'd say that." Devon's hands framed her face and he lowered his head, touching his lips briefly against hers. "Now, back to business."

Caitlin couldn't quite hide her disappointment and Devon laughed. "Is there still room at the table?"

"Of course," she said without hesitation. Understanding dawned and she rearranged the table settings in her head to include two more. "Vickie and Ned?"

"Vickie has a one-day pass to leave the center. Ned called and they should be here within the hour."

"I can't wait to meet her."

She knew that Devon had received two short letters from Vickie since she'd gone into treatment for her anorexia. Caitlin had been with Devon when he told the children about their aunt and they'd responded by adding her to their daily prayers.

"I can't wait to meet your family."

"Then why do you look so pale?" Caitlin teased. "They're going to love you."

"They're going to wonder what you see in me," Devon said, half-jokingly.

Caitlin thumped him on the chest. "That's not true. They're going to see the same things I see."

"And what would that be?"

"The man I fell in love with. Suede elbow patches and all."

"That reminds me." Devon tugged at her sleeve. "Are you ever going to give this back?"

"Nope." Caitlin danced out of his reach. "I should peel more potatoes. And make another salad—"

She reached out to adjust the taffeta bow on the banister and scooted to one side as Rosie, wearing reindeer antlers and a jingle bell collar, darted past her.

The doorbell rang and they looked at each other

"That'll be Evie and Sam," Caitlin predicted. "She's always early."

Caitlin greeted her sister and brother-in-law as they came in, weighted down with a box filled with presents. Patrick, who'd ridden over with Cade and Meghan, walked in moments later with Vickie and Ned, who they'd met in the driveway.

Caitlin and Devon took turns with the introductions, each proudly presenting their family members before everyone crowded into the parlor to catch up and watch the children enjoy the presents everyone had brought for them.

Later on, Caitlin excused herself to check on dinner preparations. After a few minutes, Devon followed.

"You know that Patrick is telling everyone that he's the reason you and I are together."

"What!" Caitlin's eyes widened. "He had absolutely nothing to do with it."

"Not from what he says." Devon grinned.

"And just what is he saying?" Caitlin demanded to know.

"The diamond ring," Devon said. "He claims that when Leona forced you to come over here that day, it gave us the opportunity we needed to talk. Oh, and I believe he mentioned something about his record being three out of three now. Whatever that means."

"Is that so?" From her position near the sink, Caitlin caught a glimpse of someone walking up the sidewalk.

Devon followed her gaze and brushed the curtain aside. "Who is that?"

"I'm pretty sure it's Leona."

"Leona Kent?" Devon blinked. "Why is she here?"

Caitlin's lips curved into a smile. "I invited her for dinner because she didn't have anywhere to go—"

"I said you are an amazing woman—"

"And because she used to teach English literature," Caitlin added smugly.

"You aren't…matchmaking?"

"Of course not." Caitlin feigned astonishment. "I'm taking my father's advice. 'Make room in your life for love,' I believe he said."

Devon grinned. "It works for me."

The doorbell rang, causing an immediate stir in the parlor.

"Someone is here!" The boys skidded into the kitchen with

Jenny close behind and Rosie barking at their heels. "Come on, let's see who it is!"

Devon took Caitlin's hand and gave her a teasing wink. "Let's see who it is."

Caitlin's heart turned over. She was still a little stunned by the depth of her feelings for Devon. Stunned, but not afraid. There'd been a few sleepless nights when she'd wondered if she could give Devon and the children everything they needed, but then she realized that was God's role not hers. What she needed to do was love them.

And loving them wasn't difficult at all.

"Dev?"

He paused and looked down at her, the smile still in his eyes. "It works for me, too."

* * * * *

Dear Reader,

Family Treasures is the final book about the McBride sisters and their treasure-hunting (matchmaking) father. I hope you enjoyed Caitlin and Devon's story. Both of them had many obstacles to overcome in order to learn to trust—and love—again.

Sometimes things that happened in our past not only weight us down in the present but can impact decisions we make about our future. Caitlin's single-minded determination to be like her mother eventually took on a life of its own and caused her to keep people at arm's length.

What an encouragement to know that God gently and lovingly offers to take those burdens from us and to reveal what is really important!

I love to hear from my readers. You can visit me at my Web site, www.loveinspiredauthors.com, or write me in care of Steeple Hill, 233 Broadway, Suite 1001, New York, NY 10279.

Until next time!

Kathryn Springer

QUESTIONS FOR DISCUSSION

1. Do you agree with the saying that first impressions are lasting impressions? Do you think it is true? Explain your answer.

2. Does the term *image* have a positive or negative connotation to you? Why?

3. How did Caitlin's and Devon's first impression of each other change over time? Did you ever meet someone and put him or her in a certain "box," only to change your mind about them later? What were the circumstances? What is the danger in judging a person too quickly?

4. Because of things that had happened in the past, Devon had a difficult time asking for help, even from his Christian brothers and sisters. What was at the root of this issue?

5. Devon saw an unlikely answer to prayer in Caitlin's unexpected presence in his life and almost rejected it because he had a difficult time trusting. Have you ever met someone and later realized that God had put them in your path at just the right time, for just the right reason?

6. Caitlin shared an embarrassing story about her adolescent years in order to let Jenny know that she wasn't alone in having feelings of insecurity. Looking into your own past, was there a similar "defining moment" in your teen years? Was it positive or negative?

7. How would you define the term *self-esteem?* Why is it im-

portant for us to look to God for our value, rather than the culture around us?

8. Think about the verse in 1 Samuel 16:7 that says "The Lord does not look at the things man looks at. Man looks at the outward appearance, but the Lord looks at the heart." As you got to know Caitlin during the course of the story, what did you see in her "heart"?

9. Just for fun, what are your favorite six pieces of clothing? Do they reflect or fit your lifestyle?

10. Devon created new family traditions with his children on Thanksgiving Day, including a piñata! Does your family have any unique holiday traditions? What are they?

11. Why do you think it was important for Devon to tell Caitlin the truth about what he did for a living? What do you think it showed?

12. What was your favorite scene in this book? Why?

13. "By wisdom a house is built, and through understanding it is established; through knowledge its rooms are filled with rare and beautiful treasures." What do you think this verse from Proverbs 24 means?

14. If someone asked you what your greatest treasure was, how would you answer?

15. How did the diamond ring the twins found ultimately help Devon tell Caitlin how he felt about her?

Love Inspired®

HOMECOMING ★HEROES★

M.A.S.H. surgeon Mike Montgomery's plans to adopt an orphaned boy from a war-torn country are squashed when he hits American soil. It seems someone else has petitioned to adopt little Ali: Sarah Alpert, the boy's foster mother—and Mike's former fiancée. And soon the adorable little boy is putting his wish for a mom and a dad into action.

Look for

Homefront Holiday

by

Jillian Hart

Steeple Hill®

Available December wherever books are sold.

www.SteepleHill.com

LI87508

REQUEST YOUR FREE BOOKS!

2 FREE INSPIRATIONAL NOVELS
PLUS 2
FREE
MYSTERY GIFTS

Love Inspired®

YES! Please send me 2 FREE Love Inspired® novels and my 2 FREE mystery gifts (gifts are worth about $10). After receiving them, if I don't wish to receive any more books, I can return the shipping statement marked "cancel". If I don't cancel, I will receive 4 brand-new novels every month and be billed just $4.24 per book in the U.S. or $4.74 per book in Canada, plus 25¢ shipping and handling per book and applicable taxes, if any*. That's a savings of over 20% off the cover price! I understand that accepting the 2 free books and gifts places me under no obligation to buy anything. I can always return a shipment and cancel at any time. Even if I never buy another book, the two free books and gifts are mine to keep forever.

113 IDN ERXA   313 IDN ERWX

Name	(PLEASE PRINT)	
Address		Apt. #
City	State/Prov.	Zip/Postal Code

Signature (if under 18, a parent or guardian must sign)

Order online at www.LoveInspiredBooks.com

Or mail to Steeple Hill Reader Service:

IN U.S.A.: P.O. Box 1867, Buffalo, NY 14240-1867
IN CANADA: P.O. Box 609, Fort Erie, Ontario L2A 5X3

Not valid to current subscribers of Love Inspired books.

Want to try two free books from another series?
Call 1-800-873-8635 or visit www.morefreebooks.com

* Terms and prices subject to change without notice. N.Y. residents add applicable sales tax. Canadian residents will be charged applicable provincial taxes and GST. Offer not valid in Quebec. This offer is limited to one order per household. All orders subject to approval. Credit or debit balances in a customer's account(s) may be offset by any other outstanding balance owed by or to the customer. Please allow 4 to 6 weeks for delivery. Offer available while quantities last.

Your Privacy: Steeple Hill Books is committed to protecting your privacy. Our Privacy Policy is available online at www.SteepleHill.com or upon request from the Reader Service. From time to time we make our lists of customers available to reputable third parties who may have a product or service of interest to you. If you would prefer we not share your name and address, please check here. ☐

LIREG08R

Love Inspired™

TITLES AVAILABLE NEXT MONTH

Don't miss these four stories in December

HER SMALL-TOWN HERO by Arlene James
Eden, OK

A job at the local motel in the town of Eden promises a fresh start
for Cara Jane Wynne and her baby boy. Her boss, Holt Jefford,
knows the secretive young woman is hiding something,
but that won't stop him from being the hero Cara Jane needs.

HOMEFRONT HOLIDAY by Jillian Hart
Homecoming Heroes

M.A.S.H. surgeon Mike Montgomery has returned to the U.S.
with a heart full of love for the orphan he saved from a war-torn
country, but his ex-fiancée Sarah Alpert is a step ahead when
it comes to adoption. Mike doesn't intend to stay for long,
but a little boy's holiday wish for *two* parents could change
everyone's plans....

MISTLETOE REUNION by Anna Schmidt

When Tom Wallace and his former wife Norah find themselves
on the same flight home for the holidays, they know their young
daughter is behind it. First a blizzard and then a house with
far too much mistletoe is all it takes to remind this family how
blessed they are.

MORE THAN A COWBOY by Susan Hornick

The identity of her daughter's father was a secret single mom
Haley Clayton wanted to keep forever. For a *very* good reason.
Yet his death has brought the truth to light. And now
Jared Sinclair, her daughter's uncle, wants her daughter
in the family for good, though it could mean that Haley
takes on a new role...as his wife.

LICNM1108BPA